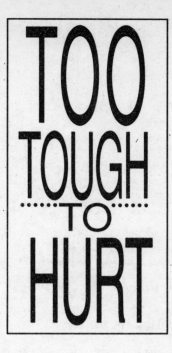

TOO TOUGH TO HURT

MARY LOU CARNEY

D1412531

ZondervanPublishingHouse

Grand Rapids, Michigan

A Division of HarperCollinsPublishers

Too Tough to Hurt
Copyright © 1991 by Mary Lou Carney
All rights reserved

Published by Zondervan Publishing House
1415 Lake Drive, S.E., Grand Rapids, Michigan 49506

Library of Congress Cataloging-in-Publication Data

Carney, Mary Lou, 1949–
    Too tough to hurt / Mary Lou Carney.
       p. cm.
    Summary: Garren's guardian angel, Herbie, helps him face many
 problems, including the separation of his parents.
    ISBN 0-310-28621-2
    [1. Angels—Fiction. 2. Interpersonal relations—Fiction.
 3. Family problems—Fiction.] I. Title.
 PZ7.C2178To   1991
 [Fic]—dc20   90-20195
                                                                 CIP
                                                                  AC

Edited by Lori J. Walburg

Printed in the United States of America

   91 92 93 94 / LP / 5 4 3 2 1

*For Brett,
my favorite wrestler*

Other Herbie books by Mary Lou Carney:

Angel in My Attic
Angel in My Backpack
There's an Angel in My Locker

Chapter

1

It was hot. One of those afternoons October throws your way like a surprise curveball. Garren and Ears leaned on the bike rack behind the school.

"Weird," Ears said, positioning his earphones. "He just up and left?"

Garren kicked at his bike tire. "Yeah. I went in the bathroom and all his stuff is gone. Toothbrush, razor, aftershave. Everything."

"So, has he called or anything?" Ears pulled a tape from his backpack and popped it into his Walkman.

Garren nodded. "From the motel last night. He tried to sound like this whole thing is no big deal, like he'd be home soon. But . . ." Garren wiped his eyes with the back of his hand.

"Hey, man," Ears said. "You okay?"

Garren nodded.

Both boys stood still in the sunshine, their shadows making long, dark marks on the sidewalk. Finally Ears said, "Gotta go. Mom's making lasagna tonight, and she'll have a fit if I'm late."

"Sure."

"Call me." Ears clicked on his tape player, flipped his skateboard down on the pavement, and kicked off toward home.

Garren swung his bike out of the rack and began pedaling as hard as he could, pumping until his calf muscles ached. Wind whirred in his ears as his heart beat hard in his chest. *Faster, faster.* His eyes stung, and he blinked against the blur of familiar houses. It wasn't until he turned the corner onto Ridge Street that Garren slowed his pace, realizing he was in no hurry to get home. No hurry at all.

Garren couldn't sleep. Lots of times in the past few months he'd had that problem—but always before it had been because the house was too noisy. His mom and dad had tried to keep their voices down—but as the arguments became more frequent, they became louder, too. Garren had covered his head with his pillow—tried not to hear. His mother's voice shrill and quick, broken by sobs. His dad's words deep and slow and angry. Sometimes the fights ended with the sound of Dad's footsteps on the stairs. In the morning Garren could see the rumpled couch where his father'd slept. Once, really late, he'd heard the garage door open and the car drive away.

But now Garren couldn't sleep because the house was too *quiet.* A thick, sad kind of silence seemed to seep up from the floors. He could hear his mother's house shoes padding across her bedroom floor. *Her bedroom,* Garren thought, *not their bedroom.* He wondered what Dad was doing. What was there to do in a cheap motel except watch TV and make trips to the ice machine? But maybe Dad had spent so many nights in motels he was used to it. He'd sure been gone a lot these last few months.

"It's my work," he'd say, whenever Garren's mom complained. "Part of being district manager for Converse means traveling. You knew that when I took this job."

"But I didn't know you'd be spending more time with your shoe samples than your son."

"How would you know? You're always running off to some committee meeting or that blasted bookstore."

And then there were the arguments about him.

"What if he gets hurt wrestling?" Mom would say.

"He's not going to get hurt! He isn't a baby, you know."

"He's my baby, and he always will be."

"You'd better worry more about that kid he hangs around with, the one who's always got those earphones plugged into his head. . . ."

Garren flung his sheets aside and got up. He began pacing his room, the arguments sounding in his head like old reruns—he couldn't shut them off.

Suddenly, he heard a tapping. Garren stopped and looked around the room. *Tap, tap.* He opened the door and peered down the hallway. *TAP, TAP.* Garren spun around. He looked toward his window. *Probably a tree branch*, he thought. Just then a bright light flashed outside, like a thousand fireflies blinking in unison. *What's going on?* Garren wondered, opening the window to investigate.

In a sudden swirl of brightness, something swooshed past Garren and landed on the windowsill. "Thanks," it puffed. "I'm not sure how much longer I could have fluttered in place!"

Garren rubbed his eyes, staring at the . . . the *thing*. Huge wings billowed from a tiny creature dressed all in white. *I'm asleep. At this very minute I'm sound asleep in my own bed*, Garren thought. *This has to be just a weird dream. Because if it isn't a dream . . .*

The creature seemed to have gained his composure. He brushed the wrinkles from his robe, straightened his halo, and smiled. Garren gasped to see that his teeth were gold. All of them! Without taking his eyes off the *thing*, Garren backed toward his door. Fumbling with the knob, he tried to open it. The creature came closer.

"Allow me to introduce myself," he said with a tiny bow.

Garren rattled the door. It was stuck fast. He looked around the room for a weapon. *Where is my baseball bat?* He grabbed his tennis racket from where it hung behind the door. Carefully, he circled the creature.

It laughed, and the sound of wind chimes rippled around

the room. "No need for that, I assure you!" And with a wave of his finger, the tennis racket sailed out of Garren's hand and back to its place on the wall. "My name's Herbekiah," he said, tipping his halo. "But you can call me Herbie. My assignments always do."

"A–a–assignments?" Garren stuttered, edging his way toward the baseball bat in the far corner.

"Yes, *assignments*," Herbie said matter-of-factly, pulling a tiny gold spiral from his sleeve. Unrolling the scroll with a flourish, he read, "Garren Gillum; Hinkle Creek Middle

School; wrestling squad; likes motorcycles and grape Popsicles and a girl named Jenny who sits by him in social studies. Lives at 1101 Ridge Street." Herbie stopped and looked up. "This is 1101 Ridge Street, isn't it?"

Garren nodded, surprised to hear that the creature knew so much about him.

"That's a relief! Once I made a mistake and showed up at a nursing home when I was supposed to go to an orphanage. You should have seen that old man's face when I told him I'd come to help him find his parents!" Herbie laughed, and the sound of wind chimes filled the room again.

Garren couldn't believe his eyes. Or his ears. *Any minute now I'll wake up.* He lunged toward the baseball bat just as it skittered across the room to the other corner.

Herbie stopped laughing. "Oh, you're awake, kid."

"How did you know I was thinking that?" Garren asked, still keeping his distance. Herbie flew around the room, inspecting everything.

"Impressive," Herbie said, pausing in front of Garren's wrestling medals.

"What do you mean *assignment*?" Garren asked, straightening a medal Herbie had bumped with his wing.

Herbie hovered beside Garren's huge stuffed spider, hanging from the center of his ceiling. "What's his name?" Herbie pointed to the furry creature.

"Samson." The word came out funny and high-pitched. Garren tried to swallow, but his throat felt the way it had that time Lynchburg caught him in a headlock.

"Actually, he looks a bit like the original one. Although of course Samson had to make do with two arms. . . ."

Garren stood looking up at the fluttering creature. Finally he asked, "You knew Samson?"

"I've known everybody," Herbie yawned. "But let's get down to business." Herbie patted the foot of the bed, and cautiously, Garren sat down. "For starters, I come from up there." Herbie flew to the window and pointed toward the starry skies beyond.

I knew it! Aliens! There's probably millions of them in my backyard right now. "From Venus?" Garren asked, fighting the panic that felt like a fist beating at his chest.

"Further."

"Jupiter?"

"Uh-uh."

"Mars?"

"Mars? Get real kid!" Herbie flew over and stood on the headboard of Garren's bed. "Have you ever seen a Martian that looks like me?"

"Well, uh, no—I guess not." *I've never seen a Martian that looks like anything!* "So where *do* you come from?"

Herbie fluttered his wings lightly. "Heaven."

Garren laughed. *Now I know I'm dreaming. All those Sunday school lessons are finally catching up with me.* "Right. Heaven."

Herbie frowned. "You don't believe me, do you?"

Garren got up and walked toward the door. "I don't have to believe you, because none of this is really happening!"

"You humans have a strange sense of reality," Herbie sighed. "You're willing to believe I'm an alien from outer space. But you won't believe I'm a heavenly creature. Why?"

Garren backed up against the door, sneaking his hand out to try the knob again. It was still stuck. "I don't know. I guess because I've seen aliens on TV—at least pretend aliens."

"Well, I'm not a *pretend* anything! I'm an honest-to-goodness, genuine guardian angel."

I really am going nuts. "Guardian angel? Whose?"

"Yours." Herbie smiled. "That's what being my *assignment* means."

A guardian angel! Garren looked at the creature. He did sort of look like those angels in nativity scenes at Christmas. And if he really were an angel, he would have all kinds of powers. Garren imagined Herbie zapping him to school every morning, doing his homework for him every night, making sure every match he wrestled was a ten-second pin. *Maybe this isn't such a bad thing after all.*

10

Herbie pulled out the tiny scroll again. "Looks like things haven't exactly been going your way lately."

Might as well play along with him, Garren thought, sitting cautiously on the very edge of his bed. "You can say that again! Dad's living in some crummy motel and Mom's crying all the time. . . ." *I'm talking to a figment of my imagination. Crazy!*

"And then there's that trouble you had with Coach after school today."

Garren turned to look at Herbie. "How'd you know about that?"

"And those new neighbors . . ."

"*What* new neighbors?" Garren asked, standing up.

"Oh, dear!" Herbie pulled a big gold calendar watch from inside his robe. "I guess I'm getting ahead of myself a bit. What with crossing all those time zones and zipping through light years and detouring black holes, it's easy to confuse one Thursday with another."

I don't have to listen to any more of this stuff. Garren got up and crossed over to the door. This time the knob turned, and he stepped into the hallway. "I'm too old for make-believe," he said, mostly to himself.

"Hey, where you going?" Herbie called, flying after him.

"To eat a bowl of cereal. Maybe a *box* of cereal. And when I get back, you'll be gone. Because I am not crazy—and none of this is really happening!"

Garren's bare feet padded down the steps. When he got to the bottom he stopped, and—slowly—looked over his shoulder and up the stairs. Nothing. Just the same flowered wallpaper and old pictures that always hung in the hallway. No aliens. No white wings. No gold teeth. Garren let out a long sigh—a sigh that couldn't quite cover up the faint, eerie sound of tinkling wind chimes coming from the direction of his room.

Chapter
2

"Pass your homework forward," Mr. Hoffer said, sipping coffee from his "#1 BOSS" mug. Outside the classroom window a row of maple trees lined the sidewalk, their colorful leaves moving back and forth in the autumn wind.

Garren opened his social studies book to the assigned pages. His homework was not there. "Oh, no," Garren moaned, leafing through his book. "Where is it?"

Ears nudged him from behind with his row's stack of papers. "What's up?" he whispered.

"Can't find my stupid homework," Garren said. He pushed his chair back, its metal legs screeching across the linoleum, and took the papers to Mr. Hoffer. "Uh, could I go to my locker?"

Mr. Hoffer looked over the top of his coffee mug. His eyes were the color of dirty river water. "Why?"

Garren felt his cheeks redden. "I . . . uh . . . can't find my homework. Maybe I left it in my locker."

"Or maybe you didn't do it at all," Mr. Hoffer said, tossing the stack of papers onto his cluttered desk.

"Yes, I did!" Garren said with more confidence than he felt.

Mr. Hoffer held out the flat, wooden hall pass. "Better come back with that homework, Mr. Gillum."

"I will," Garren mumbled as he pushed open the door. "I hope," he added to himself, hurrying down the hall.

Locker number 254. Garren banged the door open. "Come on! It's got to be here somewhere!" He burrowed through the piles of paper littering the bottom of his locker. Holding his math book upside down he shook it, hard. No homework. "I'm dead meat," he mumbled, bending into his locker and feeling in his coat pocket.

"Looking for something, kid?"

Garren jumped and hit his head on the top shelf of his locker. "Hey, what's the big idea. . . ." He stepped back and looked around. Nobody. Suddenly, the hallway was filled with the tinkle of wind chimes. "Just like last night," Garren whispered. When Garren looked in his locker again, his homework lay in a neat stack on top of his bike magazines. "Hey, that wasn't there before—or was it?" He shot a glance around the hallway. *Cripes! I'm talking to myself!* Grabbing the papers, he headed toward class.

"What, not even a thank you?" The familiar voice echoed in the empty hallway.

"Who said that?" Garren whirled around and stared down the hall. Caramel-colored lockers seemed to stare back. When he turned around, he found himself looking up into the frowning face of Mr. Hoffer.

"Talking to yourself, Mr. Gillum?"

Garren held out his homework. "No, uh, not exactly." He eased past Mr. Hoffer and slid into his seat.

Ears punched his shoulder and gave him the "thumbs-up" sign. "All right, man! You found it."

Garren took out his pencil and began copying notes off the board. "Yeah," he whispered back. "Good thing I didn't leave it at home!"

"You did, kid." Herbie sat on the end of Garren's pencil, polishing his halo with the edge of his robe.

"Ackh!" Garren yelled, tossing his pencil across the room. It rolled to a stop near Mr. Hoffer's foot. Everyone laughed. Sheepishly, Garren started forward. "Sorry," he muttered, picking up the pencil and heading toward his seat. Mr. Hoffer shook his head and continued writing.

Suddenly, there it was. The wind chimes again! "Hear that?" Garren asked Ears.

"What?" Ears said, looking up from the motorcycle he was drawing in the margin of his paper.

"Nothing," Garren sighed. Across the aisle, Jennifer covered her mouth and tried to swallow her giggles. *Great*, Garren thought. *Now she thinks I'm a real nerd!*

Garren poked at his mashed potatoes. "Looks like cold Cream of Wheat," he said. "And this mystery meat . . ."

"Hey, don't review it. Just eat it!" Ears said, shoving a piece of buttered bread into his mouth. He used his spoon to get the last few kernels of corn. "See you outside. I got to talk to this kid about his new board."

Garren sat alone, listening to the clink of forks and the rattle of trays above the constant buzz of conversation in the big cafeteria. Alone. He felt that way a lot lately, even when there were other people around. He turned as someone tapped him lightly on the shoulder.

"Excuse me, kid," Herbie said softly. "Mind if I join you?"

Garren stared at him. "You again!" He glanced around to make sure no one was watching.

"Herbekiah. We met last night, remember?"

Garren dropped his head so no one would see his lips move. "I thought you were just a bad dream."

"Quite the contrary. I'm more like a dream-come-true."

"Well, if you've come to help me make a fool of myself, don't bother!" Garren hissed. "I can do that all by myself, you know."

"Hey, about this morning, I'm sorry." Herbie leaned against the salt shaker. "Sometimes I get a little carried away. And when I saw what a stuffed-shirt that Mr. Hoffer is . . ."

Garren pushed his spoon deep into his mashed potatoes.

14

"Yeah, he's pretty straight. His idea of a good time is a matching quiz of states and capitals."

Herbie laughed his wind-chime laugh. "At least we woke everybody up. It's probably the most excitement you've had in there since L.B. Lawrence made his model Civil War cannon that shot real marbles."

How did he know about L.B.? Garren picked the frosting off his chocolate cake.

"Yes," Herbie said.

"Yes, what?"

"Yes, I'm real. That's what you're wondering. I'm as real as the food on your tray, the pockets in your jeans, and the C you're going to get on that surprise health quiz next period."

Can this guy really read my mind? Garren wondered. *Spooky!* He picked up his tray and headed for the dishwashing window. "Why me?" he asked, tossing his milk carton into the trash and shoving his tray onto the moving line.

"Why not you?" Herbie asked, following him out to the deserted hallway. "You could use a little heavenly help."

Garren looked out the window at Ears doing tricks on his skateboard. "Can other people see you?" He glanced over at the angel, who was imitating Ears's moves, minus a skateboard.

"Nope." Herbie spun in the air, turning an imaginary board.

"Hear you?"

Herbie came to a screeching stop and shook his head. "Uh-uh. Just you."

Maybe this isn't such a bad thing after all, Garren thought. *Maybe he's sort of like a fairy godmother.* "So, when do you start solving my problems?"

Herbie negotiated one last jump before hopping off his imaginary board and landing in Garren's outstretched palm. "Not bad, this skateboarding stuff. Almost better than flying."

Garren started on his wish list. "First, get Mom and Dad

15

back together. Then get Coach off my back. And I want to pin everybody in wrestling. Even at practice. Straight A's would be nice." Garren's face broke into a grin. "Hey, can you make me taller? Maybe then Jennifer . . ."

"Hold it, hold it, kid!" Herbie fluttered his wings and shook his head. "Who says I'm here to solve all your problems?"

"Aren't you?"

Just then the bell rang. The halls filled with kids pushing and laughing and shouting. "Not exactly!" Herbie yelled, gaining altitude. "But I do owe you one for this morning."

Garren looked up. "How you going to pay me back?"

"Wel-l-l-l," Herbie said, scratching his head through his halo. "How about this. . . ."

"Hi!" Garren turned to see Jennifer standing next to him. "Uh, hi."

"Didn't you think that social studies homework was just awful?" she smiled.

"Sure. Yeah. Awful."

"My next class is gym. How about you?"

Maybe this guardian angel guy is going to be cool after all, Garren thought as he and Jennifer, shoulders touching, walked side by side down the hall.

Chapter

"A shrink! You got to go to a shrink?" Ears stood in the aisle between the adventure videos. While he talked his eyes kept darting over to the large-screen TV, where a flashy Corvette was being chased down some city streets by a fleet of police cars.

"She's a counselor, not a psychiatrist. Mom and Dad have to go, too."

"Pow!" Ears smacked his hands together as two police cars collided and did a double roll. When the dust had settled, he turned back to Garren and said, "But why do *you* have to go? You're not the one getting the divorce."

"Who says anybody's getting a divorce?" Several people turned to look in their direction, and Garren lowered his voice. "It's like Mom said—they just need some time to sort things out. It's only a separation. Soon everything will be back to normal."

"Whatever you say." Ears shrugged, taking a vampire video from the shelf and reading the back cover. "But having a dad who lives at Motel 8 seems pretty far from normal to me."

"How would *you* know what normal is?" Garren teased, flicking the tiny gold earring that hung from his lobe.

"At least you can see my collar," Ears retorted, pulling the hair that hung down over Garren's neck.

"Cut it out," Garren said, knocking Ears's hand away.

"No, *you* cut it out—or should I say, 'cut it off!' " Ears laughed.

"Don't bug me about my hair!" Garren turned and walked toward the door.

"Hey, man," Ears said, following him, "I was only kidding!"

Garren stopped. He wasn't really mad at Ears. It was just that everybody seemed to be on his case lately. Mom, Coach, Mr. Hoffer. And now he had to go talk to some strange lady counselor. What business was it of hers if his family was having trouble? What could she do?

"Are we gonna get a movie or not?" Garren asked.

"How much you got?"

The boys emptied their pockets. Together they came up with enough money and began looking up and down the long shelves.

"How about one with giants and wizards and dragons . . ." Ears turned to see Garren in the far corner by the big-screen TV. He seemed to be arguing with the sheriff on the video.

"But I don't want to watch *The Heavenly Kid*." Garren was talking right at the sheriff's pot belly. "I want to watch *Motocross Mania*."

"Come on," Herbie pleaded, hovering in front of the TV. "Those motorcycle movies are so grimy and noisy."

"It's probably boring."

"Angels are not boring!" Herbie huffed.

"Uh, who you talking to?" Ears asked, coming up behind Garren.

Garren whirled around. "Nobody. Myself." He held up the *Heavenly Kid* tape. "How about this? I hear it's really good."

"And who told you that, a little birdie?"

"Sort of," Garren said, heading for the checkout stand.

"Weird," Ears said, shaking his head. "Maybe he does need a shrink after all!"

The whole office was a lifeless white—the color of the putty Dad used on the windows last spring. Rug, chairs, walls. Even the counselor, Mrs. Adney, looked putty-colored. She had wide, round glasses and bright eyes. *Too bright*, Garren thought, pushing his thumb into the upholstered arm of the chair. He looked around for a couch. He'd have to tell Ears there wasn't one—which meant she couldn't be a shrink. Everybody knew psychiatrists always had couches in their offices. Garren realized she was speaking to him.

". . . give us a chance to get acquainted." She stopped talking and looked at him.

Garren knew she was waiting for him to say something—but what? "Yes, ma'am," he said, his voice squeaky and tight.

"Now, tell me about yourself. Do you like sports?"

Garren shrugged. "Sure. I guess."

"Do you have any one sport in particular you like? Football, maybe?"

Garren thought about his favorite T-shirt. He'd gotten it at a wrestling meet last year. In big red letters it said:

Girls play basketball.
Boys play football.
Men wrestle.

He wanted to tell Mrs. Adney about it, but what if she didn't think it was funny? What if she had six boys and they all played basketball? "Football's okay," he said without looking up.

It was the longest hour of Garren's life. Mrs. Adney kept asking questions—simple things, really. But Garren didn't feel like telling this stranger anything about his life, much less his problems.

"Garren," she said, "when did you first notice your parents weren't getting along?"

It's none of your business! he thought. "I . . . I don't know." Garren was surprised to realize that this was true. He couldn't remember exactly when things had begun to fall apart, when the laughter had stopped and the coldness began filling up the silences between Mom and Dad.

Mrs. Adney asked about other things, too. His friends, his hobbies. What he liked to do in his spare time. But the words wouldn't come, and most of Garren's replies were either one-word answers or a shrug of the shoulders.

I bet she's getting mad. Garren shifted in his chair. Wasn't the hour about over?

Finally Mrs. Adney walked around and placed her hand on Garren's shoulder. "Lots of people have trouble sharing details of their lives with someone they hardly know. We'll be together every Thursday afternoon, so when—and if—you're ready to talk, I'm here to listen." She smiled. "Maybe we can sort through some of the things that are bothering you."

Garren tried to smile back.

"I'll see you next Thursday."

Garren realized it was over. He stood up and ran his hands down the sides of his jeans. *Did you thank somebody for listening to you? Even if you were paying them?* Finally he said simply, "Bye."

Once out in the hall, Garren leaned against the blue-striped wallpaper. He knew Mom was waiting for him in the lobby downstairs, but he didn't want to see her yet. He had things to think about.

"How you doing, kid?"

Garren watched Herbie flutter just below the light fixture. *Weird. My life is so totally weird. Dad's living at Motel 8. Mom's reading want ads and crying about the fact that she didn't finish college. And I'm talking to some flying creature who's supposed to be my guardian angel.* Garren pulled at a loose piece of wallpaper.

"So, did she . . . help you sort stuff out?" Herbie asked, his face serious beneath the halo.

"I've 'sorted things out' for myself." Garren faced Herbie. "It's my fault. This whole thing is my fault."

"Did she say that?" Herbie's frown got deeper. "Because if she did, I've got a thing or two to teach her!" He rolled up the sleeve of his robe and shook a tiny fist at the closed door.

"No, *I* said that. I should have been a better kid for them, Herbie." Garren walked over and pushed the "down" button on the elevator. A soft whir came from behind the closed steel doors. "You know, brought home better grades, maybe been in the school play. And I shouldn't have griped at Dad for missing my wrestling meets. Maybe if I'd taken out the trash without being reminded and done my homework . . ."

"Hold it!" Herbie said, blocking Garren's way and looking him in the eye. "It's *not* your fault. You can't blame yourself. Your mom and dad are full-grown humans, with minds of their own."

But Garren went right on talking. "And since it's my fault, I'm going to fix it."

"How?" Herbie hovered in the hallway and watched Garren step into the elevator.

"I'm not sure yet. But we'll think of something."

"*We?*" Herbie asked.

"Sure!" Garren said as the elevator doors began closing. "You *are* here to help, aren't you—"

Mom came across the room as soon as the elevator doors opened. "How was it, baby?"

Garren cringed. He hated it when she called him that, especially in public. "Okay, I guess. It wasn't so bad. She listens better than the counselor at school who makes out our schedules."

"Oh, good." Mom seemed nervous. She kept glancing around the lobby like she thought the walls might collapse at any minute. And then Garren knew why. Dad. He saw his dad push his way through the revolving door and stand looking around. Mom turned to Garren and spoke quickly. "Your dad wants to take you out for dinner. I told him to meet us here. I'll take the car and go on home." In an instant, she was gone.

Garren waved to his dad. "Over here!"

Dad smiled—that great smile of his that put creases up his jaw and made his dark brows raise. "How's that bicep?"

22

He poked Garren on the arm. "Still the fastest takedown on the team, huh?"

"Maybe." Garren shifted his weight from one foot to the other. It was creepy. Here he was, standing in the middle of an office complex lobby with his dad. The man who had taught him to ride a two-wheeler, cast for bass, do long division. So why did he seem like such a stranger?

As the smile faded, Garren thought Dad looked tired. "Got a new pair of wrestling shoes for you in the car," he said, putting his arm around Garren's shoulders and heading for the door. "Converse's latest. Split sole, metallic laces. You'll be the envy of everyone on the team." Out on the sidewalk, the sound of traffic drowned out his father's voice, but he kept on talking anyway. It was as though he was afraid to stop, afraid Garren would evaporate into the night air.

Finally they were inside the car. The backseat was filled with shoe boxes. An opened briefcase with scattered order forms was on the passenger's side. "Let me get this out of the way," Dad said, stuffing the papers inside and clicking the briefcase shut. He tossed it onto the floor of the backseat while Garren slid in and fastened his seatbelt. "So, where do you want to eat? How about Aruelios? We could have a basket of that great garlic bread you like. Or we could splurge on barbecued chicken at Wingfield's."

Garren watched the headlights streaming off the freeway. "The bowling alley."

Dad glanced sideways as he pulled into traffic. "What?"

"I want to go to the bowling alley and get hot dogs."

"Wouldn't you rather go someplace nice?"

Garren looked straight ahead. He didn't even blink. "Uh-uh."

"Okay," Dad sighed, "if that's what you want."

Light rain began to fall. On the radio, a country singer was singing some sad song. Dad clicked on the wiper blades. With their every *ker-swish, ker-swish* Garren felt the knot in his stomach get tighter. *I'm just hungry*, he thought to himself. But somehow he knew it was more than that.

Chapter 4

The crack and rumble of bowling pins filled the air. Loud laughter drifted up from the lanes as the men slapped each other on the back. "I knew you could pick up that spare! You're sure hot tonight!" Their matching shirts were bright dots of color in the smoky room.

Garren and his Dad sat at the snack bar, sipping sodas. "Two Chicago-style dogs," the waitress said, placing two huge hot dogs—with cucumbers and relish, tomatoes and onions, mustard and sport peppers and pickle spears—in front of them. "Anything else I can get you?" She chewed her gum between each word.

"No, thank you," Dad said, reaching in his wallet for a five-dollar bill. "This is fine."

Garren picked up his hot dog. How he loved these things! The first one he'd ever had was at a Cubs baseball game in Chicago. His father had taken him. "Just us two men," he'd winked as they headed onto the tollway that Saturday morning. How long ago had that been? A year? Two? It seemed longer.

"How's school?" Dad asked, picking the peppers off his hot dog.

"Same as always, I guess."

"Getting straight A's?" Dad teased.

"Not in this lifetime!" Garren finished his soda and made

a loud slurp with the straw. That always drove Mom crazy, but Dad hardly seemed to notice. "Might get an A in wood shop, though. Mr. Trzeciak says my stool looks good. He might even put it in the display case in the hall."

"That's good. Real good." Dad poked at his hot dog.

We should have gone to Wingfield's, Garren thought.

Dad signaled for the waitress and got them two more sodas.

Two Cokes. Usually his Dad had a fit if he didn't drink milk for dinner. But that was the old Dad . . .

"Son," Dad said, clearing his throat, "about this separation." A loud whoop came from the lanes, followed by clapping and cheers of "Strike! Strike!"

Garren felt the food in his mouth grow clammy. He didn't want to talk about the separation.

"I'm sure you've noticed that your mom and I haven't been getting along so well these past few months."

"Everybody fights. It's no big deal." Garren shoved his straw deep into his ice.

"But not every day, day after day." Dad's voice had a sadness to it that Garren had never heard before. "It's just not *right*. That's no way to live."

"And Motel 8 is?" Garren asked, glaring at his Dad.

"No, of course not."

Garren swallowed around the lump forming in his throat. "Then come home. Mom misses you. I know she does. And I . . ." Garren felt a quiver creeping into his voice.

Dad reached over and put his hand on Garren's shoulder. "I can't, sport. Not right now. Maybe the counselor will help us. Help us all." Dad shook Garren's shoulder playfully. "I forgot to even ask you about your session. How'd it go? Does Mrs. Adney seem like a nice lady?"

"Sure. I guess." Garren pushed the rest of his hot dog aside. "I've got a wrestling meet tomorrow after school. Home."

"Going to make weight?"

"No problem. I've been wrestling up the last few weeks

anyway, getting ready for conference competition." *Please say you'll come. Please.*

"Sorry I can't make it to your match," Dad said, placing a tip on the counter. "I've got this meeting with our distributor in Westville, and I'll be lucky to get back by seven."

"It's okay," Garren said, sliding down off the stool. Inside, he wished it really were okay. He'd never gotten used to not having someone in the bleachers to cheer for him the way most of the other kids did. Even when Mom wasn't working at the bookstore, she didn't care much for wrestling meets. Sometimes Ears came, but not often.

"How about a Dairy Queen?" Dad asked as they walked across the parking lot.

"No, thanks," Garren said. Suddenly he wanted very much to be standing in his own room, surrounded by his own things. He wanted to feel the way he'd felt before any of this had happened. He wanted to go home. And as he watched Dad drive down the familiar streets, he wondered if he felt the same way.

Garren undressed in the dark, enjoying the familiar shapes in his room. Bed. Dresser. Medals. A faint light glimmered on top of the bookcase. Herbie.

"Have a good time, kid?" The light seemed to pulse as Herbie spoke.

"Yeah, sure. The best."

"Everything all right with your dad?"

How should I know? "Uh-huh. He brought me this great pair of wrestling shoes." *I don't even know who he is anymore! Why does everything seem so strange? Even the hot dogs tasted different!*

Suddenly the room vibrated with sound, like a train passing at close range. Herbie's light grew brighter and brighter, until Garren squinted and put up his hand to shield against its brilliance.

"Hey, what's the big deal?" Wrestling medals clanked

and papers flew around the room. Garren's huge stuffed spider swung back and forth like a leaf in a hurricane.

"The big deal is that I'm tired of your not leveling with me!" Herbie sailed around the room, knocking books off shelves and scattering a stack of clean underwear.

"What are you talking about?" Garren yelled back. "I answer all your stupid questions, don't I?"

Herbie pulled up short right under Garren's nose. Slowly, he dimmed, and Garren thought he could feel the slight breeze from the beating of his wings. "Listen, kid. It's me. Your *guardian angel*. Not some chump counting out your change at Burger King and telling you to have a nice day. I *care* about you."

Garren turned down his bed and crawled beneath the covers. Herbie's light grew even softer, like the night-light Garren had had in his room when he was little. "Can you really tell what I'm thinking?" Garren whispered.

"Yep."

"Even the bad stuff?"

Gently the wind chimes tinkled. "Even the bad stuff. But don't let it worry you. Nobody's perfect—at least nobody this side of heaven."

"It seems weird—having a . . . a guardian angel. I'm not sure what to say to you."

"Say anything you want. I'm here to listen, mostly. And help out some, too."

Garren sighed, and the light came closer. "It was awful, Herbie. Dad seemed just like a stranger."

"Tell me about it."

And Garren did.

Chapter 5

The moving van was big and orange. Its diesel roar woke Garren up on Saturday morning, and for an instant, Garren thought that Mom was moving out, too. Relief warmed his insides like hot chocolate after sledding when he realized the van was parked next door, at old Mr. Norris's place. Except it wasn't Mr. Norris's anymore. His daughter had come a few months ago and taken him to live in a retirement home. Shortly after that, a "For Sale" sign had gone up in the yard.

"I hope a family with a dozen boys moves in next door," Garren had said to his mother. "Our neighborhood's too full of old men walking dogs and ladies hanging out diapers. You can't even get up a decent game of ball around here!"

"Maybe a beautiful young lady will move in," Mom had kidded him. "And she can become the 'girl next door' who steals your heart away."

"Fat chance!" Garren had laughed, grabbing an apple from the fruit basket and heading out the back door.

Now a moving van was here. Maybe it *would* be a family with boys! Garren watched out his window as the men began unloading things. Beds and dressers. Table and chairs. The furniture looked old, antiques maybe. Mom would like that. Then there was a piano. "Come on," Garren whispered. "Unload some *boy* stuff—a few dozen baseball bats or a fiberglass backboard."

"Spying on the new neighbors?" Herbie asked, yawning and stretching. He'd spent the night curled in the palm of Garren's baseball mitt.

"No, just their stuff. I haven't seen any people yet."

Garren turned away from the window to look at Herbie. He was beginning to get used to the idea of having a guardian angel. It seemed almost natural, somehow. And Herbie *was* a good listener.

"They look dull, don't they?" Herbie asked, flying over to the dresser mirror to examine himself.

"The new neighbors?"

"My teeth! You were staring at my teeth! I knew this would happen." Herbie pulled back his top lip and examined his teeth. "How can an angel be expected to keep a first-class shine on them with all this carbon monoxide and factory smoke and . . ."

"Your teeth look fine," Garren said. He yanked open a dresser drawer and grabbed a pair of sweats.

"You're just saying that." Herbie perched on top of the lamp. He pulled a small, sparkley bag from his sleeve. Unzipping it, he took out a tiny gold toothbrush and a roll of shiny floss. "Maybe a few thousand strokes with the brush and a thorough flossing."

"Go ahead, Herbie—have a good time. I'm supposed to meet Ears at McDonald's." Garren pulled on his faded blue sweatshirt. "See you after breakfast. Maybe our new neighbors will show up by then."

"I'll start with five hundred strokes on the incisors," Herbie said. "One, two, three . . ." The tiny toothbrush moved up and down, up and down, up and down.

Garren and Ears sat on Garren's front steps, sucking on grape Popsicles and staring through the chain-link fence to the yard next door. The moving men went from the truck to the house and back again, like wind-up toys on a track.

"So, where are the people?" Ears asked, punching the EJECT button on his player and turning the tape over. He readjusted his earphones and pushed PLAY.

Garren shrugged. "Who knows!" He was getting tired of waiting. Maybe if he and Ears tossed a few balls, the boys next door would come out to play. If there were any boys.

"Maybe they're not really *people*," Ears said, doing his Freddie Krueger laugh. "Maybe they're zombies and can only come out after dark. Or maybe they're werewolves and are waiting for a full moon."

"I don't care what they are as long as they've got a few good outfielders."

Just then the window on the side of the house opened. It made a creaky kind of sound. Garren and Ears looked toward it. A shape, concealed behind the dingy white curtain, stood staring at them.

"Suppose that's one of them?" Ears whispered.

"Must be," Garren said, turning to watch the men in the moving van pull away from the curb.

When he looked back toward the house, the figure was gone.

"I'm still hungry," Ears said, standing up and starting inside. "Got anything—"

Just then a man came out of the house next door. He was bent over, as though he were walking into a stiff wind. He wore a brown suit that had a shiny, wet look to it. In his hand he carried a tan felt hat with a black band. Before the boys could even speak, the strange man was standing in front of them.

"Excuse me, young man," he said, his voice raspy and gruff. He kept running his thumb around the brim of the hat. "I find myself in need of making a call and our phone is not yet installed. Could you be so kind?"

Garren stared at the man. What a queer neighbor! And he'd said *ours*. Did that mean there was someone else over there? Was that the shape they'd seen? Ears elbowed Garren in the ribs, bringing him to his senses. He jumped up and opened the door. "Sure, of course. Use ours. My mom's not home right now; she went to the grocery." Garren and Ears followed the man into the family room, where Garren pointed out the phone.

The man turned to look at them. "I'll only be a moment. Local call, I assure you."

Garren realized he wanted them to leave. "Great. No problem. We'll just wait on the porch."

Ears pushed Garren out the front door. "Are you crazy? Letting a perfect stranger into your house, telling him your mom is gone, leaving him alone in there!"

"I wouldn't say he was *perfect*," Garren said, cupping his hands against the glass and looking through the window. "But I'd sure say he was strange! Besides, what was I supposed to do? He's my new neighbor, remember?" Garren turned away from the window. "He's coming! Try to act natural."

"We *are* natural, man. It's him . . ."

They shut up quickly as the man came out the door. "Thank you, I'm sure," he said. He hurried down the sidewalk toward his own house.

"You're welcome!" Garren called after him.

"I'm sure!" Ears added, both boys choking to keep their giggles inside.

"Did you meet the new neighbors?" Mom asked later as she and Garren unsacked the groceries.

"Almost." Garren carried the milk and orange juice over to the refrigerator.

Mom stopped with a can of soup in each hand. "How can you almost meet someone?"

"Ears and me saw a shape behind one of the curtains." He shoved the stuff inside and closed the refrigerator door with his foot. "And then a man came over and used the phone."

"What was his name?"

Garren realized he didn't even know. "Beats me. He just used the phone and left. Pretty weird guy, if you ask me."

"Well, nobody asked you." Mom frowned. "They're our new neighbors and we're going to make them welcome."

"I was afraid you'd say that," Garren sighed, opening the freezer door. He put the three boxes of grape Popsicles where he could get to them without having to move the frozen broccoli.

Garren pushed the little white button. Inside, the sound of the doorbell echoed on and on. *Maybe nobody's home,* Garren thought. He switched hands; the casserole Mom had made was still warm. He rang again. A dusky kind of darkness seemed to wrap itself around the house, and shadows lurked behind the untrimmed shrubbery. Garren was just turning to leave when he heard the bolt slide. Slowly, the heavy brown door opened. There stood a girl about Garren's age. Her hair hung down on her shoulders, almost covering her face. She stared at him with the greenest eyes he'd ever seen.

Garren swallowed hard. "Hi, my name's Garren. We live next door. My mom—"

Without waiting for him to finish, the girl grabbed the casserole and slammed the door. Garren stood there, stunned. *Great. The weirdo father has a weirdo daughter. Just what the neighborhood needs!*

"Were they home?" Mom asked Garren as he came in the door.

"Oh, they're home. Let's just hope there's not a full moon tonight."

"Now what's that supposed to mean?" Mom called as Garren bounded up the steps to take his shower.

When Garren got out of the bathroom, Herbie was sitting on his bed, reading a comic book. The pages turned by themselves. "So how was your day, kid?" Herbie looked up. Garren had on the old pair of gym shorts he always slept in—and sunglasses. "Sunglasses?" Herbie asked, frowning.

"It's those teeth!" Garren said, holding his hands in front of his eyes. "The shine is blinding! Incredible! First class!"

Herbie laughed, and the sound of wind chimes rippled around the room. "Cute." Garren took off his sunglasses and tossed them on his dresser. "Seriously," Herbie said, "do you think they look better?"

Garren flopped down on the bed on his belly and got so close his nose almost touched Herbie. "Absolutely."

Herbie closed the comic book. "So, what do you think of your new neighbors?"

"Strange. Kooky. I'd rather have old Mr. Norris back, even though he did have a fit every time my ball landed in his yard."

"Kind of a snap judgment, isn't it, kid?"

"Hey, Herbie, I know a loser when I see one—and we've got two of 'em living next door. The man wears suits that look like they came off a Goodwill truck and talks like he's got a clothespin on his nose. And that girl!" Garren grunted. "Rude. And funny-looking. She wouldn't even speak to me when I took her Mom's casserole—and I rang the doorbell ten minutes before she even answered!" Garren rolled out the rag rug he kept under his bed and began doing pushups.

Herbie perched on his shoulder. "Things aren't always what they appear to be."

"Oh . . . yeah?" Garren puffed. "That's what I thought . . . about Mom and Dad . . . that it wasn't as bad . . . as it looked." He lay flat on his stomach, his face pressed into the rug. "But it was. It was as bad as bad could be." Herbie hopped off his shoulder, and Garren shoved the rug back under his bed and clicked out the light. He lay on top of the covers, his heart beating hard.

Slowly, Garren began to relax. Maybe things would get better between Mom and Dad. After all, they were all going to that counselor, weren't they? And he prayed—every single day—that things would be like they used to, that they could be a real family again. He thought about the new family next door. Where was the mother? Was she as weird as the rest of them? *Tomorrow*, he thought, snuggling into his pillow. *I'll ask Herbie about it tomorrow.*

Chapter

6

Garren poked at the macaroni on his plate. He was tired of macaroni. This was the third time this week they'd had it. He noticed Mom wasn't eating, either. If she didn't like macaroni, why did she make it all the time?

"I went to see a lawyer today. His name is Mr. Babcock."

Garren dragged the prongs of his fork across the plate. It made a loud, squeaky sound—like a hundred nails run across a chalkboard.

Mom kept talking. "He's drawing up the separation agreement."

"Was Dad there?"

Mom shook her head. "He has his own lawyer."

Garren pushed back his chair from the table. He carried his plate to the sink and dumped his rubbery macaroni down the garbage disposal. "What kind of agreement is it?"

"Well, your father will pick you up after school every Wednesday and take you to dinner. Then he'll drop you off for youth group at church. I'll pick you up." Mom followed him to the sink.

"What about weekends?" Garren tried to keep his voice steady. *This is stupid! A kid's supposed to be able to see his dad any time he wants!*

"You'll spend every other Saturday with him. On Sundays, you and I will go to church, and then your father will have you Sunday afternoon and evening." Mom put her arm around Garren. "Look, baby, I know this is hard on you. It's not easy on me, either."

"Then why are you doing it?" Garren looked his mother in the eye. She was pretty. When he was little, he used to love those parent days at school so everyone could see how pretty his mother was. Now, for the first time, he noticed the little wrinkles around her mouth. And there were dark circles under her eyes.

"I told you. Your father and I can't get along. We want different things from life."

"And what about what *I* want? Doesn't anybody care about what I want?" Garren felt his voice getting louder.

"Everybody cares about you." Mom began loading the dishwasher. "That's the most important thing."

"If you really cared about what I wanted, you wouldn't have thrown Dad out of the house!" He was screaming. He was screaming at his own mother.

Garren could see the hurt and then the anger in her eyes. "Nobody threw anybody out. He wanted to go—to be with his precious shoe samples and his briefcase. All he thinks about is work, work, work."

Garren felt like his insides were being torn in half. He wanted to defend his dad, to scream it wasn't so. But he remembered all those dinners Dad never came home to eat, all those school activities he missed. "Oh, Garren's father had to work," Mom would smile, trying to be interested enough for two. But then, she'd never understood Dad—how important it was for him to be the best. Garren could understand; that's how he felt about wrestling. But how was he supposed to choose sides?

"Speaking of work," Mom said, dumping in the dish-washing powder and closing the door, "I asked for more hours at the bookstore. Lucky for me, one of the girls will be starting maternity leave next week. But I'll have to work some Saturdays. Maybe even evenings."

"Why?" Garren hated the thought of coming home to an empty house, of becoming one of the "latchkey" kids he read about in his news magazine in social studies.

"We need the money, Garren."

Money. He'd never even thought about that. "Isn't Dad giving us money anymore?"

"Of course. Some. But he has his own expenses now, too."

Are we going to be poor? Will we start buying my clothes at the Salvation Army store? Garren remembered the macaroni. *Will we ever have stir-fried shrimp again?*

"Definitely the blue one." Herbie perched on top of Garren's dresser mirror, watching as Garren pulled out shirt after shirt, rejecting one after the other.

Garren held up a striped rugby against his chest. "I've got to look cool for this picture, Herbie. Last year my shirt was straight out of 'Leave It to Beaver.' "

"Trust me, kid. I've been around for a long time. I've seen togas and robes, tights and capes, bell-bottoms and tie-dyed and punk. Wear the blue."

Garren laid the blue shirt on top of his favorite faded jeans. "I guess you're right," he said. "Now if my hair just won't stick out all over. . . ." He smoothed back his wet bangs and stood looking at himself in the mirror. He had his father's chin and his mother's nose. Everybody said so. But his eyes were his own. For an instant, Garren thought of the girl next door with the green, green eyes. He sat down on his bed and began thumbing through his literature book, looking for the assigned story.

"I'm sure she will."

"Huh?" Garren still couldn't get used to Herbie knowing what he was going to say before he said it.

"I'm sure Jennifer will want to exchange pictures."

Garren smiled. "Hope you're right."

"Guardian angels are always right!"

"Hey, Herbie, have you ever had *your* picture made?"

Herbie shook his head. "I am what you'd call *unphotogenic*. Truly unphotogenic."

"Mom takes a great picture. Always has." Garren closed his book. "Want to see some pictures of me when I was little?"

"Sure, kid."

Garren came back with a stack of photo albums. Together he and Herbie curled up against his pillows. He opened the first one. "That's Mom and me coming home from the hospital."

"You're the bald one, right?"

"Uh-huh." Garren laughed. They turned the pages. "And here I am with my first fish. Dad was so proud. I was only four—and I landed him myself." There were other pictures, too—trips to the beach, their vacation to Disney World, birthday parties and Christmases. On the very last page was a wedding picture of Garren's parents. He looked at it for a long time. "They look happy, don't they?"

"They were."

"So what happened, Herbie?"

Herbie's wings drooped a bit. "Lots of things happened, kid. Hurt feelings and harried work schedules; disagreements and broken promises; angry comments and wounded pride."

"Words, Herbie. All those things are just words." Garren touched the wedding photo. "Was it me? Were they only happy until I came along?"

Herbie flew up in front of Garren and paced back and forth in midair. "Are you kidding?" He waved his arms as he talked. "When you were born, your folks were so happy they could hardly stand it! Your mother called everyone she knew, and your dad was stopping total strangers in the hospital corridor to show them his new son. They brought you home to teddy bears and mobiles and picture books— and a brand new two-wheeler. Your dad said he just wanted to make sure it was there when you were ready for it."

Herbie sat back down next to Garren. "No, kid, it wasn't you."

"Then what?"

"Things change. You're not exactly bald anymore, and you've long since outgrown that two-wheeler your dad bought when you were born. And while you were changing, your folks changed, too."

"Was it Dad's job, Herbie?"

"Not just that. There were a million other things. Your mom and dad grew in different directions. They wanted different things from life. And they forgot to make time to really listen to each other. Slowly, they became interested in separate things."

"And now they've got their very own *separation*." Garren was about to toss the stack of albums aside when he had an idea. "Hey, I know! I'll find a picture of us all—a happy picture taken before the yelling began. Then I'll give it to Dad when he takes me to dinner. He'll see us all together and remember what fun we had. And on the way home we'll stop by Motel 8, and he'll pack his suitcase and come home with me. We can go back to being a real family! And Mom and Dad won't ever even think about divorce again." Garren flipped through the albums, looking for just the right picture.

"I'm not sure that's such a good idea. . . ."

"This one's perfect! Warren Dunes. We'd been swimming all morning and had just eaten this great picnic lunch Mom packed. Then Dad and I played Frisbee in the water. Mom kept applauding every time I caught it. It was a perfect day, Herbie. Perfect. Dad will remember—he has to." Garren peeled back the corner of the page and gently pulled the picture loose. His folks were kneeling on the beach, the wind tossing strands of hair across Mom's face. He stood between them—his bare foot propped up on his sand bucket, his arm crooked to display a tiny muscle. And they were all smiling like crazy.

Garren looked at it for a long time before he turned off the light and laid the snapshot on his bedside table. *Wait till Dad sees this. Everything's going to be okay. Everything's going to be okay.* Garren let the words echo in his mind as he drifted toward sleep.

Chapter 7

"I can't even see!" Garren said, pulling at his rubber mask until the slits were even with his eyes.

"Yeah, but you look great!" Ears adjusted the lump on his back. "These stupid towels keep slipping. I'll be the only hunchback in town with a hump under his armpit."

"Let's pull the belt tighter." Garren reached under the big flannel shirt and slid the buckle into the next notch. "There, that ought to hold it."

"Tha-a-ank you wery much!" Ears said as he hobbled around the room, dragging his right leg.

"We'll never even get to the end of our block if you walk like that!"

"You're right." Ears straightened up and ran in place, lifting his knees until they almost touched his chin. "My leg is healed! It's a miracle!"

"No," Garren laughed, "it's greed. You want to get as much candy as you can."

"Vhy not?" Ears said, holding open the pillowcase he'd brought along. "Trick or treat!"

Garren tossed in a handful of tiny candy bars from the dish on the table.

"Now you boys be careful." Mom came into the family room carrying two huge bowls of bubble gum and peanut butter kisses. "Remember, just go to the houses here in our neighborhood. And don't eat anything until you get home so I can check it."

"Gee, Mom," Garren mumbled through his mask. "You'd think I'd never been trick-or-treating before. Aren't you going to tell me to look before I cross the streets?"

"Okay," Mom said, "look before you cross the streets." Garren shook his head. The big mask made everything sound hollow, and it smelled like the mattress covers at camp. "Remember, the newspaper said you're only allowed to trick-or-treat from 6 to 8 P.M."

"Ees all right, Mizzez Gillum," Ears said, holding out his fake hand with long, black nails. "I turn into somezing awful at 8:01 anyvay."

"Yes," Garren's mom sighed, "I know—a seventh-grader."

Grabbing another handful of candy bars, the boys ran out the door.

The air smelled of fog and burning leaves. Shadowy forms of witches and ghouls and ghosts flitted up and down porch steps.

"Think we're too old for this stuff?" Garren asked, stepping off the sidewalk so a mother and her clown-faced child could pass by.

"Naw," Ears said, unwrapping one of the candy bars and popping the whole thing into his mouth. "We're just the right age—big enough so no one will try to steal our candy and young enough to still get treats."

The boys rang doorbell after doorbell. They cut across yards and scuffed through leaves. Their pillowcases got heavier and heavier. One old man gave them nickels. A couple of houses didn't have their porch lights on, but Garren could see the glow of TV sets inside. "Some people are so cheap."

"Yeah," Ears agreed. "We ought to come back tonight with about a zillion rolls of toilet paper. . . ."

Just then a group of trick-or-treaters rounded the corner.

They were about the same size as Garren and Ears. They, too, were dragging heavy pillowcases. "Hey, look at those two *creepy* characters!" the girl in front giggled. She was dressed as a cheerleader and wore a tight sweater—one that bulged in all the right places. Garren tugged on his mask and tried to get a better look.

"Go-o-od e-e-evening," Ears said, going into his limping routine and circling the group. They all began to scream and laugh. "Vhat are you doing out on dis terrible night?"

"Trick-or-treating, same as you."

Garren recognized the voice as K.C.'s, a girl from his Carney school. Probably they were all from Hinkle Creek.

"Got anything good in your bag?" the cheerleader asked, edging toward Garren.

It was Jennifer! Garren held open his bag. "Take something. Anything."

Jennifer leaned over, brushing her sweater against his arm. "I think I'll take . . . this!" She pulled out the big Snickers bar Mrs. Jones had given him. Garren wished she had taken the apple instead, but he didn't say so.

"Bye!" the girls called. "Don't stay out too late!"

The boys watched them disappear down the street.

"Did you get a look at Jennifer?" Ears whistled.

"Yeah," Garren said as they headed for the next house. "She sure didn't look like that at school today!"

"And with our luck, she won't look like that tomorrow, either."

"Maybe it's just the full moon that made her look so . . . full!" Both boys laughed. It felt good to laugh. Garren realized he hadn't been doing much of it lately.

It was after eight when the boys turned the corner onto Garren's street. Their bags were so full that they carried them flung over their shoulders, Santa Claus style. Ears had given up on his hump and it lay in a crumpled pile at his waist. Garren had pushed his mask up on his head.

"We've hit every house in our neighborhood," Garren said.

Ears stopped and put his hand on Garren's chest. "Not *every* house."

"Name one we missed!"

"Your neighbors. The 'creepy twosome.'"

It was true. They hadn't trick-or-treated the new neighbors. In fact, Garren hadn't even seen either of them since last Saturday and the telephone/casserole ordeals. He looked down the street now and saw that their porch light was on.

"I don't know. . . ."

"Aren't afraid, are you?" Ears teased. He put his hands under his armpits and flapped his arms, squawking like a chicken. "Garren's chicken! Garren's chicken!"

Garren walloped him with his full pillowcase. "Am not. It's just that, well, we've got enough candy. And I bet they don't have any good treats anyway."

"Who cares about the candy? Let's *scare* them."

Garren and Ears stopped in front of Garren's house and stood looking across the fence.

"How?" Garren asked.

"I'll ring the doorbell like a nice little trick-or-treater. You hide behind that tall bush next to the porch. When they come out to give us some candy, you start moaning and groaning."

Garren smiled. "And I can get louder and louder."

"Then jump out with your mask on."

"I've got an idea. Wait here." Garren ducked around to the side of his house. In a minute he was back, carrying a big bottle of ketchup.

"What . . . I get it!" Ears laughed. He opened the ketchup and poured it on Garren—all over his hands, down the front of his shirt, and finally over his head. It slid down his mask in globby, red streams. "It looks like blood! It really does! This is going to be so cool!"

The boys struggled to keep from laughing as they sneaked next door. Garren crawled behind the bush. Ears waited until Garren gave him the sign that he was ready. Then he sauntered up the sidewalk and rang the doorbell. Nothing.

He rang again. He waited. *Bring-ing-ing-ing*. Ears let his thumb rest on the bell. Finally, the door opened with a slow creak. Garren began moaning, growing louder and louder. The girl with green eyes stepped onto the porch, holding a bowl of candy. She didn't seem to notice the moans. Ears had to almost yell, "Trick-or-treat!" The moans increased, blood-curdling and nearby. Still the girl stood on the porch, holding out the bowl. Finally, Garren jumped out of the bushes. She whirled around. He was still moaning and groaning, stumbling across the porch and into the railing. "I think he's been stabbed!" Ears said to her. "He may be dying!" The green eyes blinked once or twice. Then she went back inside, the door slamming behind her.

Ears couldn't believe it. She hadn't even flinched! Garren lay draped over the side of the porch, still moaning. "Forget it," Ears said, pulling his arm and getting him on his feet. "We struck out."

Garren stopped moaning and pushed up his mask. "Maybe she's used to bloody, groaning bodies." He shrugged.

The boys hopped over the fence into Garren's yard just as the neighbors' lights went off.

But as Garren turned to wave good-bye to Ears, he noticed the girl had stepped back onto her porch. She stood silently in the shadows, watching his house. *Weird*, Garren thought, shivering as a cloud passed over the moon.

Chapter 8.

"Bridge, Gillum! Arch that back! Pretend there's a hundred-pound opponent on your chest and you're not about to let him pin you!" Coach's face was as red as the wrestling mat he stood on. His neck aching, Garren dug his heels deeper into the mat and pushed. He wondered how Coach Cannon could yell so much and still have a voice left.

The *trill-lll-llum* of Coach's whistle echoed off the padded walls of the wrestling room. "Listen up, men!" he shouted. One by one the boys stopped their warm-ups and came to sit crosslegged in front of Coach. His "Hinkle Creek Wrestling" shirt stretched across his broad chest and flat stomach. Huge biceps pushed against the short sleeves. Flipping through the papers on his clipboard, Coach began his pep talk.

"We've got to get in shape! Be tough! Too tough to hurt! I'm going to run you until you don't know what winded is, until you can go the distance. If you don't get them in the first round, you can get them in the third when your opponent's sucking air and you're feeling fine."

Garren made sweaty palm prints on the mat. He'd heard it all before—a hundred times before. Be quick. Shoot deep. Protect your back. Never let 'em know you're hurting. Make your opponent wrestle *your* way. But this was the year he had to make it all work for him. And so far he had. Four

45

meets, four wins. 4–0. By the end of the season, Garren wanted a 15–0 record. He *needed* a 15–0 record. Then he'd be "Most Valuable Wrestler" and Mom and Dad would come to the banquet together and remember how things used to be and . . .

"Right, Gillum?"

Garren could feel Coach's hot breath as he bent over him. *Right what?* he wondered. Everyone was looking at him. "Yes, sir," he said, trying to make his voice deep. "Right!"

Coach seemed satisfied and moved on to his next point. That was close! He'd seen guys have to do two dozen push-ups or—worse yet as far as Garren was concerned—run ten laps for not paying attention. More and more lately Garren found it hard to pay attention. In class. At practice. Even in church his mind was always wandering, always trying to find the solution to this stupid separation. Or at least the reason for it.

"—so how tough are you?" Coach asked, ending his speech with the usual challenge.

"Too tough to hurt!" the team yelled together.

The whistle sounded again. "Pair up for live wrestling!" Garren squared off with his partner, Mosier. Mosier was a good ten pounds heavier than Garren, but Garren liked it that way. Then when he faced kids his own size in the meets, they seemed light as marshmallows. Coach walked from mat to mat, yelling out criticisms and an occasional compliment. When he got to their mat, Garren gave it all he had. He and Mosier faced each other, their foreheads almost touching. Then, in a flash, he dropped to one knee and shot deep, taking Mosier by surprise. Mosier landed on his back. Garren was on top of him, working the half, trying for a pin. Mosier's neck muscles strained as he arched and fought against Garren. Garren caught his neck in the crook of his arm and tugged. Coach slapped the mat. "Pin!"

Mosier rolled aside and kicked playfully at Garren. "You'd have never gotten me if I'd been ready."

"You should be like me," Garren smiled, gasping for breath. "I was *born* ready!"

Soon practice was over. "Hit the showers!" Coach yelled. "And remember to watch your weight! We got two meets next week." Garren wondered if macaroni and cheese was fattening. "You, Gillum!" Garren turned around. "I want to talk to you."

The other boys filed past on their way to the locker room. Garren could hear the sounds of their laughter from inside. *What now?* he thought, slipping his arms out of his singlet and walking toward Coach. All he could think about was how good that cool shower spray would feel on his sticky body.

"Been having a decent year so far, huh, Gillum?"

Garren shrugged. "Pretty good."

"Don't be modest!" Coach said, slapping Garren's behind with the clipboard. "You've pinned every opponent."

What does he want me to say?

"You could have a great year. Maybe your best."

It's got to be my best.

"Except for one thing." Coach spoke these last few words slowly, the anger apparent in every syllable.

"What one thing?"

Coach exploded. "Your hair! How many times have I told you to get it cut? You look like a girl, Gillum. You want to wear a ponytail? Go out for volleyball or cheerleading. But on my team we look like men!" Coach thumped on the clipboard. "Every one of us!"

Garren could feel the wetness of his hair on his sweaty neck. So his hair was a little long—it was his hair, wasn't it? What right did Coach have to tell him how to wear it?

"You're not going to go on the mat looking like that! We have rules in wrestling, rules to keep our men looking like— men! What's next, Gillum? Eye shadow? Lipstick?"

Garren made his hands into fists. He could feel his fingernails digging into his palms. He knew if he said one word, he'd be running laps until he was forty years old.

"Do it my way, Gillum. Get a haircut. If not, you'll find yourself standing beside the mat instead of wrestling on it!" Garren stood there, biting his lip. Biding his time. Slowly, Coach's face began to lose the red blotches. He shook his head and said, more quietly than Garren knew possible, "Hit the showers."

The locker room was almost empty. Only a few guys were left, lacing up their shoes, tossing dirty socks into gym bags. Grabbing a towel from his locker, Garren slipped out of his singlet and stepped into the empty shower room. There was no hot water left, but he didn't care. For several minutes, Garren stood beneath the spray—letting the water massage his aching muscles, inhaling the familiar smells of sweat and soap and mildew. Maybe if he stayed in here long enough, he could wash away his problems, too.

By the time Garren finished his shower, he was alone in the locker room. He pulled on his sweats and stood in front of the big mirror, combing his hair. His hair. Who'd have thought he could get in so much trouble just by growing a little hair? It lay in wet strands on his neck, touching the hood of his sweatshirt.

"It's *my* hair!" Garren said aloud, snapping his comb into the mirror.

"That it is, kid." Herbie balanced himself on the end of the faucet and looked up at Garren.

"And it's nobody's business how I wear it!"

"Hmmm," Herbie said, flying up on Garren's shoulder and looking at him in the mirror. "I wouldn't say that. . . ."

"I'm not getting it cut."

"Tell me something. Why this sudden interest in long hair? You've never even let it touch your ears before."

Garren shoved his singlet and shoes into his bag. "It looks good like this. Besides, lots of professional wrestlers have long hair." He stopped and looked up at Herbie. "Even Samson had long hair!"

Wind chimes tinkled. "True, true! But you see, the

Philistines had no rules about that sort of thing. And middle-school wrestling does."

"I'm sick of people telling me what to do! When to eat and when to go to bed. What to read and where to ride. How long to stay on the phone. Which days I can see my dad." Garren kicked open the locker-room door. "Rules or no rules, Herbie, I'm not getting it cut. And Coach can't make me."

"Well," Herbie said as they started down the stairs, "Lynchburg will be glad to hear that."

Garren stopped. "Lynchburg?"

"Sure. If you don't wrestle, he'll be conference champ for sure."

Garren thought about this. Lynchburg. Conference champ. No undefeated season. No "Most Valuable Wrestler." No awards banquet with Mom and Dad sitting next to each other. Garren threw his bag over one shoulder as he grabbed his bike out of the rack. "Well, maybe I'll trim it just a tiny bit with Mom's sewing scissors. But nobody else is cutting my hair!" Garren jumped his bike off the curb and turned toward home.

"That's just what Samson said, too!" Herbie yelled, hanging onto the handlebars with one hand and his halo with the other.

Chapter 9

Garren dragged his rake through the scattered leaves. November. *The armpit month of the year*, he thought, pulling stray leaves from the chainlink fence. He looked next door. What good would it do to rake the yard if the neighbors let their leaves pile up waist high? The next big wind would blow them back over his yard.

Just then the door opened and the green-eyed girl stepped out on her porch. Garren leaned on the handle of his rake and watched her. Odd. The whole thing was odd. Why didn't he ever see her at school? And why didn't she answer him when he yelled across at her? Then there was that Halloween episode.

"Hi," Garren said. No response. The girl was bent over some yellow flowers growing at the end of the porch. "Sure are lots of leaves to rake, huh?" Nothing. Garren kicked at the rake and wished for the thousandth time that some normal boy had moved in next door. He was just about to begin raking again when he saw Ears coming down the sidewalk. He was riding his skateboard and—as always—listening to his tape player. He was really booking! Every time he came to a place where the sidewalk was uneven, Ears would bend his knees and make the skateboard fly up in the air. The *whirr* of wheels and the *whack* of jumps broke the chill air.

Suddenly Garren realized that the girl had stepped out onto the sidewalk. She was staring down at something— something moving. A woolly worm. *I hope Ears misses it*, Garren thought. Ears got closer and closer, riding faster and faster. The girl didn't move. She was smack in the middle of the sidewalk, and Ears was too busy watching for tree roots and cracks to notice. *Move. Why doesn't she move?* Before he realized it, Garren had jumped over the fence and run to where she was kneeling. He grabbed her out of the way just as Ears whipped past them, looking up in surprise.

"Hey, man, I'm sorry!" he said, stepping off his board and coming toward them. "I didn't even see you."

She was shaking. Tears filled her green eyes. For the first time Garren noticed how pretty her hair was—long and soft and full of blond streaks. With a grunt, she pulled her arm away from Garren and ran into the house. Both boys stood watching.

"You're welcome!" Garren yelled, hopping back over the fence and picking up his rake.

"Want to go down to the arcade?" Ears asked, carrying his skateboard into the yard.

Garren shook his head. "Have to get all these leaves raked."

"Bummer."

"No kidding."

Ears shuffled his high-tops. "I didn't see her, man. I really didn't."

"Forget it," Garren said, dragging a section of leaves into his pile. "You know, you're getting pretty good on that thing."

"Practice makes perfect!" Ears laughed. "Least that's what my mom told me the whole three months she made me take piano lessons." He plopped his board down on the sidewalk. "Later, man!"

"Sure!" Garren said, watching Ears coast across the street.

Garren had almost finished raking when he heard the banging of the truck doors. Two men in a city truck got out at the end of his street. They were putting up some kind of sign. Stuffing the last of the leaves into the bag, Garren walked down to see what was happening. The men took a yellow sign out of the truck. The sign said, in big black letters, Deaf Child Area.

Garren laughed. "Hey, you guys must be mixed up. I've lived here all my life and there's no deaf child around here."

The bigger man stopped his work and looked at Garren. "No mistake. Town board approved it last week. Ridge Street. Deaf kid." The men pounded the pole into the ground and attached the sign to it. Soon they were finished, and the truck pulled away.

Garren walked over and touched the sign. They'd probably be back before dark to take it down. Deaf child in area? What deaf child?

Slowly he turned toward home, kicking through piles of leaves. They crackled and whooshed as he scuffed along the curb. Twilight sifted through the bare trees, turning everything a soft, sad blue. Deaf child. What would it be like to be deaf? To be swallowed in silence all the time? Garren thought about Ears—he couldn't live without his music. And what about TV shows? And telephone calls? The wind began to pick up, flinging stray leaves against his jeans. *You couldn't even hear the wind.* For a moment, Garren stood still and listened. The sound of a distant train. The rhythm of a car engine as it passed. Wind whistling overhead. *It sure would be weird to be deaf!* he decided, hurrying through his front gate.

A movement from next door caught his eye. It was *her* picking up the evening paper from the porch. *If she weren't so weird, I'd go over and tell her about the sign, about the mistake. There's no deaf child around here!*

And then it hit him. The sign had gone up *after* she'd moved in. She'd acted like she didn't even hear his screams on Halloween night. And why didn't she know Ears was barreling toward her on his skateboard? The girl next door. Was it possible? Could she be . . . deaf? That would explain a lot of things. An awful lot of things.

Garren reached for another piece of chicken. If Dad were home, they'd have had to use real plates. But tonight he and Mom just ate right out of the big striped paper bucket. This was his third leg. Used to be he had to share the legs with Dad. "Only decent part of a chicken," Dad always said. But now Garren could have them all. He stared at his piece of chicken and wondered what his dad was having for dinner.

Maybe cheese crackers out of the hotel vending machine. Suddenly Garren realized he wasn't so hungry anymore.

"Sorry I had to work late," Mom said, nibbling at her cole slaw. "We're already getting in extra stock for Christmas. I must have unboxed two hundred books today!"

"And I must have raked two million leaves," Garren said, throwing his paper plate into the trash. "Whose idea was it anyway to fill our whole yard with trees?"

Mom wiped her mouth with her napkin. "Your father's," she said slowly.

Too bad he's not here to help rake them! Garren thought.

"I finally met our new neighbor today," Mom said, wrapping the leftover chicken in foil.

Garren swallowed hard. What did Mom know about the girl?

"He's a widower. Just moved here from Wheatfield. Teaches at the university. Philosophy, I think."

"What about . . . *her?*"

"Oh, yes. The daughter. About your age, poor child."

"Poor child?"

"She's deaf. Quite deaf. Has been for several years. One of the reasons they moved here was so she could go to the county co-op's school for the hearing impaired."

Deaf. The green-eyed girl was deaf. Garren had never felt like such a jerk in his whole life.

"Tell me about her, Herbie," Garren said. He pulled off his back bike tire and began working his way around the rim with a screwdriver.

Herbie hovered above an oil spot on the garage floor. "What do you want to know?"

"Everything. Her name for starters."

"Her name's Elise. She's thirteen years old. She plays the piano and writes poetry and throws a pretty mean spitball."

"But she's *deaf*, Herbie!" Garren popped out the tube and began patching a slit.

"And she's deaf," Herbie said.

"Why didn't you tell me? I thought she was just, you know, *weird*."

"As I recall, I tried to tell you about snap judgments. . . ."

Garren shoved the tube back into the tire and worked it onto the rim. He pushed on the air pump, watching the tire get fat again. "I feel like a real creep."

"I can understand that."

"She must hate me. Really hate me."

"No," Herbie smiled, "as a matter of fact she thinks you're kind of cute."

Garren stopped pumping. "Really?"

"A little strange, but definitely cute."

Garren checked the pressure and pushed his bike back against the wall. "So what do I do now? If I ring her doorbell again, she'll probably think I'm just going to play another stupid joke. And how can I explain things to her if she can't hear me?"

"Just because she can't hear doesn't mean she can't communicate, can't understand. She knows sign, does some lip reading—and can read words *quite* well." Herbie picked up a paintbrush lying on the workbench.

"What do you have in mind?"

"Remember the posters you made when Jennifer ran for student council? The ones you put all over the school lawn?"

"Yeah," Garren laughed. "She won, too."

"Well, you have some cardboard and stakes left. . . ."

"I get it!" Garren grinned.

It was way past his bedtime when Garren slipped across the fence and into the yard next door. Under his arm he carried three big signs. As quietly as he could, he drove the stakes into the frosty ground. He made sure Elise could see them as soon as she looked out the door in the morning.

"Now what happens, Herbie?"

Herbie's halo glimmered in the moonlight. "We get some sleep, kid and—just like with the elections—we wait and see."

Chapter
10

When Garren woke up the next morning, the first thing he did was look out his window and into the neighbor's yard below. The signs were still there. He could read them even from here.

SORRY
ABOUT-
THINGS.
Garren

I'M NOT TOTALLY
WEIRD-ONLY
A LITTLE
WEIRD.

HI!! I'M THE
KID WHO
LIVES
NEXT DOOR.

The last one had been the hardest to write. And now that he read it, Garren was afraid Elise would misunderstand. When he wrote *things* he'd meant . . . he wasn't sure exactly what he'd meant.

The stupid Halloween prank for sure. And the sarcastic way he'd yelled, "You're welcome!" But what if Elise thought he meant her deafness? What if she thought this was some warped attempt at humor? Or pity?

"Herbie," Garren said, "maybe this was a dumb idea. What if—"

Just then the front door opened and Elise stepped out on the porch. Garren raised his window and pressed his nose against the screen. She stood with her back to him for what seemed a long time. And then—Garren was sure of it—he heard Elise laugh. A bubbly, giggly kind of laugh. Then she hugged her arms around herself and twirled across the porch, her hair whirling out around her shoulders like a blonde parasol. On tiptoe, she ran across the icy yard and yanked up the signs one by one. Just before she went back inside, Garren thought he saw her glance toward his house.

There. It was done. Now what? Would she think he was even more queer than before? Or maybe—just maybe— she'd want to be friends. So what if she were a girl? And deaf. Herbie said she could throw a great spitball, didn't he?

School seemed to last forever. Ears was absent and lunch was chipped beef and Mr. Hoffer gave a surprise current events quiz in social studies. Garren had made up his mind. Tonight, after dinner, he would go over to see Elise. He'd take that little chalkboard he'd tossed up in the top of his closet years ago, the one he used to practice his times tables on.

"It'll seem strange to write notes instead of talk to her," Garren said to Herbie after school as he reached for his homework.

"Just pretend you're in homeroom," Herbie laughed, the

tinkling of wind chimes echoing inside the locker. "You've had a lot of experience writing notes in there!"

When Garren got home, there was a piece of paper taped to the front door with his name on it. At first he thought it was from Mom—but she always hung her messages on the refrigerator door with little strawberry magnets. Slowly, Garren unfolded it and read:

> A young girl once lived next door
> To a boy she just couldn't ignore.
> From Halloween pranks
> To notes nailed on planks—
> He certainly wasn't a bore!
>
> _Elise_

Next to her name was a smiley face with green Magic-marker eyes.

"Not a bad limerick!" Herbie said, reading over Garren's shoulder.

Garren waved the note at Herbie. "This is great," he laughed. "I'm going over there right now."

Herbie shook his head. "Not home. The bus from the school for the hearing impaired drops her off at the university and she rides home with her father after he finishes teaching his five o'clock class."

"Oh." Garren sighed, carefully folding the poem and putting it in his back pocket. "Guess I'll just wait until after dinner, then." He looked across the fence into Elise's yard. "And while I wait, I might as well rake a few leaves." He tossed his books inside and reached for the rake propped up against the house.

"There you are!" Mom waved from the back door. "I got home from work and couldn't find you anywhere in the house." She looked at the yard next door. "What a nice thing to do!"

"Uh . . . well, it's just so they won't blow back over on

our side of the fence," Garren said, heaping up another pile of soggy leaves.

"Right, kid," Herbie said. "And you only kept that note from Elise because you don't like to litter!"

Garren patted his back pocket and kept raking.

It was so cold Garren's breath came out in little frosty puffs. Shivering, he pulled the collar of his jean jacket up around his neck. He looked at her porch light. *Is she expecting me?* Garren wondered. The little slate was tucked under his arm. Taking a deep breath, Garren rang the doorbell. *No wonder it takes her so long to answer the door. How does she even know it's ringing?*

Just then the door opened. The green-eyed girl—Elise— smiled at him. "Hi!" Garren waved. "I live next door!" He pointed next door. He realized he was shouting. *Dumb.* Elise motioned him into the living room, where her father sat grading papers. He stood up when Garren walked in.

"Good evening," he said, reaching out his hand. "I don't suppose we've officially met. I'm Mr. Peterson, Elise's father."

"Uh . . . nice to meet you." Garren took the hand and shook it. It felt like a limp fish. He was glad when Mr. Peterson let go. "I'll leave you two children to yourselves," he said, gathering up his papers and starting up the stairs. "Do sit down."

Garren slid into the closest chair. *Children. Sounds like something my mom would say.* He watched Elise as she tossed another log on the fire and poked it into place. Tiny sparks shot up like Fourth-of-July fireworks. Garren took out the slate. What should he write? He balanced it awkwardly on his knees. Elise sat down on the couch and motioned for him to come sit beside her. Garren did, and Elise reached for the slate.

MY NAME IS ELISE, she wrote. I GO TO THE SCHOOL FOR THE HEARING IMPAIRED IN TOWN. I HAVE AN INSECT COLLECTION, A TEN-SPEED BIKE, AND

A FATHER WHO THINKS I'M BREAKABLE. She smiled and underlined the last word.

Garren laughed. "Yeah, my mom feels the same way. If I'm—" He stopped mid-sentence. He erased what she had written and wrote: I'M GARREN. I GO TO HINKLE CREEK MIDDLE SCHOOL. I HAVE A DIRT BIKE AND TWENTY-TWO WRESTLING MEDALS AND A MOM WHO CALLS ME "BABY." He underlined the last word and Elise smiled. *Did I only imagine I heard her laugh?* Garren wondered. *Can she talk?*

DID YOU RAKE OUR YARD? she wrote back.

Garren nodded.

THANK YOU. Elise began sketching something with her chalk. It was a skateboard. She looked up at Garren and raised her eyebrows in a question.

"My friend, Ears," he said.

She looked puzzled, then pulled on her own ear.

Garren laughed. "Yes, Ears!"

Elise underlined the THANK YOU and drew a line to the picture.

"No problem," Garren said. He fingered his chalk awkwardly.

Erasing the board, Elise wrote: WOULD YOU LIKE SOMETHING TO EAT?

Garren shrugged. "Sure," he said.

Together they went into the kitchen. Elise poured them each a glass of root beer. Then she reached into the freezer for—Garren could hardly believe it—grape Popsicles!

When Garren finally left, Herbie was waiting on Elise's front porch. His wings were resting against the column at the end of the railing and he was flossing his teeth. "So, how'd it go?" Herbie asked, stuffing the gold floss into a pocket deep inside his robe.

"Okay."

"Only okay?"

"Better than okay." Garren smiled as he started down the sidewalk toward home. "It's weird, Herbie. I keep forgetting she can't hear. She seems so . . . normal."

60

"She *is* normal, kid. She likes to window-shop at the mall and read scary stories and play cards."

Garren laughed. "She beat me at Uno five times!" He paused at his back door and looked across to the freshly-raked yard. Elise's porch light clicked off. "Does it hurt to be deaf, Herbie?"

Herbie hovered in the moonlight, his wings barely moving. "What hurts most is when others don't understand, when they treat deaf people as though they aren't whole individuals. Or when they just avoid them altogether—like they have bubonic plague or something." Garren yawned and reached for the door handle. "Hey," Herbie said, flying around and perching on his shoulder. "Did I ever tell you about the time I was in Europe—this dumpy little village in France—I think it must have been six, no—seven hundred years ago? The plague was everywhere and there was this one old man. . . ."

"Here, Herbie," Garren said, handing Herbie the slate and pushing open the back door, "write it down and I'll read it in the morning." Then, laughing, Garren bounded up the steps to his room—feeling so happy that for just a minute he forgot about the separation. And it felt good to forget.

Chapter

11

"So, tell me about your week."
Mrs. Adney took off her glasses and leaned toward Garren.
Outside her office window the clouds hung low and gray.

What was there to tell? The Wednesday-night dinner with
Dad—a dad he hardly knew anymore. An argument with
Mom about that D in home ec. Another threat from Coach
about his hair being too long. And a truly stupid argument
with Ears about who was the best major league hitter. *Just a
typical terrible week*, Garren thought. He stared down at his
shoes. They were scuffed. And one shoelace was beginning
to ravel. When had that happened? Bending over, he
touched the fraying end. *Falling apart—just like my life.*
Garren could feel Mrs. Adney looking at him, but he
couldn't bring himself to look up, much less talk. What good
was talk anyway? They'd been coming here for almost two
months now. Had it gotten Mom and Dad back together? It
was a dumb idea, telling some stranger your problems. He
heard Mrs. Adney stand up and walk to the window.

"Look at that sky! We'll get snow tonight for sure, don't
you think?" Garren shrugged his shoulders. "How about a
cola?" she asked.

"Sure," Garren mumbled into his shirt collar.

Garren held the can of Coke so tightly he could feel the
sides denting in. The only sound was the ticking of the gold

clock over the door. *I should say something. This is costing Mom money.* But his tongue felt big and awkward. Garren took another sip of pop, letting the biting fizzle linger in his mouth. Then, suddenly, Mrs. Adney began talking.

"Once, when I was a little girl, my father took me fishing. I soon got tired of holding the pole and swatting mosquitoes, so I decided to go wading in the creek. I had barely gotten my feet wet when I stepped on a broken bottle. The glass dug deep into my foot, and blood spurted into the water. I screamed and screamed, even after my father had removed the glass and bandaged the wound." Garren looked up. "I still have the scar." She smiled, wiggling her high-heeled foot. She paused, and the smile faded. "And once, when I was in sixth grade, my best friend had a slumber party." Garren tried to imagine Mrs. Adney as a sixth grader. "At least I thought of her as my best friend. But she didn't invite me to her party—and to this day I remember the giggles and whispers of the other girls the day of the party. I remember how left out and miserable I felt. And I never told anybody. That scar's inside here," she said, tapping her chest.

Garren nodded his head. "When I was in first grade," he said, swallowing the last of his pop, "I was always the last one picked for teams. I tried to hide in the bathroom every day during gym—but I never told my teacher why."

"You know," Mrs. Adney said softly, "when you're hurting, it's hard to open up and talk about it. Somehow you're afraid you'll be hurt even more. But that's not the way it is," she said, coming around her desk and sitting next to Garren. "Talking doesn't double your trouble; it cuts it in half."

Garren sighed. He was for anything that would get rid of some of his problems. "It's been a rotten week," he said.

And Mrs. Adney settled back to listen.

"Why doesn't Elise talk to me?" Garren sat at the kitchen table, dabbing white polish on the ends of his sneakers. "She *can* talk, can't she, Herbie?"

"Why don't you ask her?"

Garren slipped on the shoes, tucking the frayed lace inside his hightops. "Why don't you just tell me?"

"Because some things it's better to find out for yourself."

"You know what I think?" Garren said, jabbing his arms into his winter coat.

"Yes, but tell me anyway if it'll make you feel better."

"I think you're a poor excuse for a guardian angel. Look at the mess my life's in! My folks are separated. I almost never see my dad. Mom works about a zillion hours a week. Coach Cannon hates me. And I'm probably failing home ec. Exactly what are you 'guarding' me from?"

Herbie fluttered down and faced Garren. "Nobody promised you life was all cupcakes and ice cream, kid. Not me. Not anybody. I'm here to help you through the hard spots, not to zap you into some twilight zone where everything is just the way you want it."

Garren felt his eyes filling with tears. *Tears! I'm thirteen years old and crying!* He ran out the back door, slamming it behind him.

The snow had started. Big, fluffy flakes like the kind inside those Christmas scenes you shake. Already everything wore a sheen of white. Garren sat on the step and watched his jeans accumulate flakes. A blue twilight made the falling snow look even whiter. Then, faintly at first, Garren heard something. The wind? Or was it words? He listened closely. They were words, but whose? He looked around for Herbie, but he was nowhere in sight.

There it was again! Louder this time. He noticed movement in the yard next door. It was Elise. She was moving among the snowflakes, doing a sort of dance. And she was talking!

> *"Snow's first flakes flutter*
> *on my face.*
> *Unheard melodies move me*
> *with an icy grace."*

She said the words again and again, dancing a circle in the fresh snow, lifting her face to the avalanche of flakes.

So she *could* talk! The voice was raspy and low and—different. *Why doesn't she ever speak to me?* Garren wondered. *I'm sick of writing on that stupid slate.* He watched her for a long time, until she at last became silent and stood staring at the few stars that had wiggled their way through the clouds. When she spoke again, it was a familiar rhyme:

> *"Star light, star bright.*
> *First star I see tonight.*
> *I wish I may, I wish I might . . ."*

Garren found the wishing star. "Have the wish I wish tonight," he whispered. And then, closing his eyes, he wished harder than he ever had before in his life. Because no wish had ever been this important.

When he opened his eyes, Elise's yard was empty. Had he imagined it all? Sometimes he felt like he was going crazy. Crazy people saw stuff all the time that wasn't really there, didn't they? But what about those footprints in the snow?

Tomorrow. Tomorrow he'd find out for sure.

Chapter 12

The whirr of the film projector sounded in Garren's ear like a million mosquitoes. A narrator's voice droned on and on about the size of China, about the important mountain ranges, about the daily diet of the people. *Who cares?* Garren thought, shifting to a more comfortable position and resting his head on the back of his chair. He closed his eyes and thought about last week's wrestling match. It had been a close one. Too close. Lynchburg had almost pinned him in those last few seconds. Garren had won on points after two overtime periods. But he could still hear Lynchburg's words as he walked, sweat-soaked and winded, off the mat. "I'll get you at conference. . . ."

When Garren opened his eyes, the film had stopped and everyone was looking at him. What had happened? He shook his head and tried to remember. Then he noticed his social studies book lying in the middle of the aisle. He must have knocked it off when he fell asleep! He reached for it, feeling the back of his neck redden. *Geek!* he thought to himself. A soft giggle rippled up from the class. Mr. Hoffer flipped on the lights and looked directly at him. *After-school detention for sure. What will Coach say?*

But Mr. Hoffer only cleared his throat and walked to the front of the room. "As I'm sure you noticed," he said to the class, "many of the facts in this film are somewhat dated. Nevertheless, it provides an excellent background for our studies. . . ."

He's going to let it slide, Garren thought. *But why?*

Soon the bell rang for the end of the period. "Pages 194–206 for tomorrow," Mr. Hoffer called. Then, as Garren gathered up his books, he said, "I'd like to see you for a moment, Garren."

Here it comes. Garren tried to look unconcerned. Why give Hoffer the added enjoyment of watching him sweat? He stood in front of the desk, waiting.

When the room was empty, Mr. Hoffer spoke. "I've been going over the grade book, Garren, and your test scores aren't as high as they usually are. You've always been a good student, and if you need extra help now . . . well, I'm here after school every day." He shuffled his papers and cleared his throat. "That's all, Garren."

Ears was waiting just outside the door. "I thought I'd bust a gut when you knocked that book into the aisle and then snored. You actually *snored!* So how bad is it, man? Horrible Hoffer give you a detention or what?"

"He's flipped out, Ears. He told me if I needed extra help, to come in after school. Said I was a good student." Garren shook his head and laughed.

"Come on," Ears said as they walked down the hall toward their lockers. "What'd he really say?"

"Honest. That was it. He even called me *Garren,* not Mr. Gillum like he always does."

"Weird." Ears gave his lock a spin and jabbed the middle of the door with his knee. It popped open with a *whang.*

"That's for sure." Garren tossed the social studies book inside his locker and reached for his home ec folder. It *was* weird. And very unlike Mr. Hoffer.

Garren was sitting in home ec, copying notes on kitchen safety off the overhead, when it hit him. He knows. Mr. Hoffer knows about the separation! Why else would he be so nice to me? But who told him? Garren felt his mouth go dry

67

and his stomach tighten. Who else knew? He looked around the room. Did everybody know that his folks were separated? That his father lived at Motel 8? Did they know he saw a counselor every Thursday? What if somebody asked him about it? What would he say? How could he explain it to anybody when he didn't even understand it himself? He felt as though everyone were staring at him, whispering, "That's Garren Gillum. His father moved out. His parents are going to get a divorce, you know."

Suddenly, Garren was on his feet and heading for the door.

"Is something wrong?" Mrs. Balta asked, stopping in the middle of a word as she wrote on the transparency.

"Uh . . . I don't feel so good."

"Do you want a pass to the nurse?"

"No," Garren said quickly. "I just need . . . a drink of water."

Mrs. Balta nodded her head and went back to writing.

Garren hurried past the row of lockers and toward the drinking fountain. Mr. Hoffer knew. They all knew. Every embarrassing moment he'd ever had paraded itself through his head. His first day of school when he'd gotten on the wrong bus to go home. That time in third grade when he'd thrown up all over his desk. Last year when Ears pushed him into the girls' bathroom. Nothing could compare with this. He felt like one of those freaks at the county fair. Broken home. Single-parent family. Divorce. Why did it have to be this way? He pounded his fist against the cold hardness of the block wall.

"Hey, kid."

Garren looked up. Herbie sat on top of the last locker, his wings moving gently back and forth. "Mr. Hoffer knows, doesn't he?"

Herbie nodded. "All your teachers do."

Garren whirled around and stomped down the hall. Herbie flew after him. "How?"

"Your mom called the school."

"Great! It's not enough that she's ruined my life at home. Now she starts on school, too!" Garren stood at the drinking fountain, twisting the knob on and off. He bent and drank with great gulps.

"It wasn't exactly a plan to ruin your life," Herbie said when Garren finally stopped drinking and stood up. "She just wanted them to know in case you needed a little extra support in the next few weeks."

"Support?" Garren said. "I don't need support—I need my dad back, Herbie. I need two parents together in one house. I won't take pity from people like Mr. Hoffer. And I don't want everybody in school to know my personal business."

"Look, kid, it's not like you've got leprosy or something. Over a million kids a year go through the same thing you're facing. Remember last year when Ryan's mom got a divorce? And what about—"

"Shut up!" Garren hissed fiercely. "They're *not* getting a divorce. Mom and Dad will get back together—just wait and see! As soon as I win 'Most Valuable Wrestler'—"

Just then the bell sounded, and the halls filled with kids. Herbie tried to sit on Garren's shoulder, but Garren shrugged him off.

"Garren, wait up!" Jennifer pushed her way up to Garren. "Thought you were in home ec."

"I was. But I came out for a drink and . . . well, never went back."

Garren could feel Jennifer looking at him. "You okay?"

"Oh, I'm wonderful. Things couldn't be better." Garren bit his lip. Hard.

"I heard about your parents. I'm real sorry."

Garren watched the frayed end of his shoelace dragging down the hall. What had she heard?

"I remember when my folks split up. It hurt plenty."

Garren looked up. "*Your* folks? But—"

"I live with my real mom and my stepdad. I was only in second grade when my parents got divorced, but I still remember how much it hurt." Then, so softly he could hardly hear her, Jennifer added, "Sometimes it still hurts."

"Well, my folks are just separated," Garren said, louder than he'd meant to. "They're probably—almost for sure—going to get back together."

"Great, that's great." Jennifer smiled, letting her hand rest for a moment on Garren's arm before she disappeared into the math room.

After school Garren and Ears stopped by McDonald's. "I found out why Hoffer is being so nice to me," Garren said to Ears. They were sitting in their favorite booth, sharing an order of french fries.

Ears dragged a fry through the catsup and dropped it down his throat. "Why?"

"He knows my folks are separated. Probably all the kids know, too." Ears kept eating. Sometimes he could be so dense! "Don't you know what this means?"

Ears licked catsup off his fingers. "What?"

"It means I can't face them, that's what. Suppose they start asking me questions about . . . things."

"Hey, man, lots of kids don't live with both parents. It's no big deal."

"Well, it's a big deal to me! How'd you like it if your parents were thinking of splitting up?"

"I just meant it's nothing you have to be ashamed of, like having lice or something." Ears reached over and pulled at a strand of Garren's hair. "Of course, if you do have lice . . ." he said, his voice getting louder. "Lice! This kid has lice!"

Garren swung across the table, but Ears ducked. "Why, you . . ."

Ears stuffed the trash in the container and dashed out the door—with Garren after him. Laughing, they ran until their chests ached from the cold air and the bright blueness of the sky seemed to swirl around them.

Chapter

13

Garren and Elise brushed the snow off the swings and sat down. Garren liked the park best in winter, when everything looked so different and there weren't a zillion little kids running all over. He grabbed the chains—cold even through his gloves—and began pumping. Higher and higher, the cold air grabbing at his chest with each *swoosh*. Elise did the same. Soon they were swinging so high the chains rippled with each tug back toward the ground. Finally, they let themselves slow, dragging their feet until brown grass began showing through the fresh snow.

"That was fun!" Garren laughed. Elise smiled and nodded. She was getting pretty good at reading Garren's lips now. And she was trying to teach him some simple signs. She raised her hands and, slowly, made the movements that said, "I love snow."

Garren looked into her green eyes, made even brighter by the red coldness of her cheeks. "I know. I saw you last night." For a moment Elise looked confused. Then her eyes widened—and she looked away. Gently, Garren pulled the chain of her swing to turn her toward him. "And I *heard* you, too." Elise pulled away, twisting the swing so her back was to him. Garren circled around her and plopped down in the snow at her feet. He looked up at her. "Why won't you talk to me?"

Her eyes were filled with tears. She pointed to herself, then her lips, and made an ugly face. Now it was Garren who looked confused. She did it again, her movements angry this time.

"You think your voice is ugly?" Garren asked. Elise nodded, and two tears slid down her cheeks. "You don't know what ugly is!" Garren said. He puffed out his cheeks, crossed his eyes, stuck his thumbs in his ears, and wiggled his fingers. When he couldn't hold his breath any longer, he deflated his face and said, "Now that's ugly!"

Elise kicked snow on him.

"Hey!" Garren yelled, grabbing a handful and tossing it into her hair. Soon the fight was on—and before long both were covered with snow. Tiny crystals hung on Elise's lashes. "Enough! Enough!" Garren howled as Elise stuffed a handful of snow down his collar. And then Garren heard it. Elise laughed. Soft and deep.

Garren sat back on his heels and stared at her. "You can talk, can't you?" Sighing, Elise nodded. "Those words you were saying in the snow, are they a song?"

Elise shook her head.

"A poem?"

She nodded.

"One of yours?"

A hesitation this time, and then again the nod.

Garren stood up and brushed off his jeans. "They were good. Really. Even Herbie says your poems are . . ." A tiny crease formed in Elise's forehead and she raised her eyebrows in question. He shook his head and waved his hand. "Forget it. Nobody." He reached out and helped Elise to her feet. They walked toward home, the cold wetness beginning to soak through to their insides. But still Elise wouldn't say one word.

They parted on the sidewalk in front of their homes, Elise signing, "Good-bye."

Garren trudged around the house to the back door. Inside, he stripped off his wet clothes and took them downstairs to the laundry room.

"Why won't she talk to me, Herbie?" Garren threw his jeans across the line, where Herbie, doing his best tightrope-walker imitation, bobbed up and down.

"She's afraid her voice sounds . . . well . . ."

"Ugly," Garren finished.

"Ugly," Herbie repeated. "When she was little, they used to visit her grandfather in a nursing home. He was deaf, and whenever he talked to them his voice was loud and coarse. It always scared Elise a little, and now she's afraid her voice will sound the same way."

"But it doesn't. It's different, but it's not so bad. And it sure beats chalk!"

"Tell her," Herbie said.

"Maybe I will," Garren answered, wrapping himself in a towel still warm from the dryer. "Next time I see her."

"The fire feels good," Garren said, stacking a black checker on Elise's king. Elise nodded. They had moved the board close to the warmth of the fireplace. Outside, it had started to snow again. With her next move, Elise took three of Garren's checkers. "I quit!" he said playfully. "No use playing the 'checker hustler of the midwest'!" Elise smiled and gathered the checker game back into its box. She reached for the slate.

Garren put his hand over it. "Talk to me."

Elise pushed his hand away and wrote, in big letters, I CAN'T.

"Yes you can! I heard you!"

MY VOICE, she wrote.

"Your voice isn't bad—or ugly." Garren set down his cup of hot chocolate. "Remember what ugly is?" he asked, sticking his fingers in his ears.

Elise nodded and smiled. She erased the slate and began writing. MY GRANDPA WAS DEAF AND—

Garren took the chalk and she looked up. "I know all about your grandfather. And believe me, you don't sound anything like that."

Elise signed, "I don't understand."

Garren broke the piece of chalk. Then he broke the pieces. He tossed the handful of pieces into the fire. Elise watched it melt into the flames. When she turned back to him, Garren couldn't make out the look on her face. Anger? Relief?

She licked her lips. A half-cough sounded from deep inside. Then, taking a big breath, she said, "Why?"

She talked! Garren laughed. "I knew you could do it!"

She talked slowly, without looking at him. "I . . . I don't like to talk to people. Since I lost my hearing, my voice . . . is . . . weird. I know it is." She looked up at him, scared.

"How do you know?" Garren asked, slowly, so she would get every word. "Have you heard it lately?"

Elise shook her head.

"Well, I have. It's different—but a nice kind of different."

Elise frowned, as though trying to think how to say what she wanted to say. "But I don't know how loud . . . am I talking loud?"

Garren shook his head. "Nope." She seemed relieved. "But if you do, I'll just do this." Garren pulled on his earlobe. "And you'll know to be a little softer."

"Grandpa was always so loud . . . how did you know about Grandpa?"

"Uh . . . got any more hot chocolate?" Garren asked, standing up and starting toward the kitchen.

For the next hour he and Elise sat at the kitchen table and talked—really talked. She told him about her old neighborhood and how much she missed the way the sun used to shine into her bedroom every morning. "When I was little, I'd pretend the sun's rays were angels, come to be my playmates for the day." She told him about how her hearing just seemed to drain away, like dishwater. "Some days it would be like all the sounds were wrapped in cotton. I loved playing the piano, but by the time I was in third grade it was

74

getting harder to hear. I could feel the ivory keys under my fingertips, but the melodies were broken, somehow. Father always accused me of daydreaming if I didn't hear what he said. And some days I *could* hear! But those days became fewer and fewer. And there were the constant colds and earaches. It almost became too much trouble to try to catch the sounds that others heard so easily. I used to hope the teacher would write the assignment on the board so I could read it. I was embarrassed to admit I couldn't hear.

"Finally, Mother began home-schooling me. At first I missed the other kids, but I was so relieved not to have to pretend I knew what was being said. And Father was glad not to have to deal with the teachers anymore. Mother and I learned signing just for fun. At first. But as the sounds became fewer, more blurred, we depended on it whenever we went to the grocery or for walks. She helped me learn to read lips, too." Elise stopped for a minute, as though so much talking had made her tired. Then she said, quietly, "Then came the accident. A farmer with a truck full of grain ran a stop sign and . . . and killed her. That was a year ago." Elise pushed her marshmallows to the bottom of her cup with her spoon. "A year and four months and six days ago."

"I'm . . . I'm sorry," Garren said.

"Father was in a daze for months. He almost lived at the university. I stayed at home and cried a lot. The next year was a nightmare. Father tried to home-school me, but it was no use. Father had no patience. When summer came, I thought he would go crazy. Roaming around the house. Standing for hours in Mother's flower garden. Then, suddenly, we were moving. 'A fresh start,' he called it. A new job for him. A new school for me." Elise scooped the marshmallows up and ate them. "But a school for . . . deaf children." She walked to the sink and dumped out the rest of her hot chocolate. "So here we are."

"Well, I—for one—am glad," Garren said, placing his empty cup on the counter.

"I guess I'm glad, too."

"And I'm glad three!" Herbie said, appearing on the windowsill over the sink. He laughed, and the sound of wind chimes tinkled and clinked in the air.

Elise froze, her eyes darting around the kitchen. Gently, she touched her ear. "I . . . I thought I heard something . . . something that sounded like—"

"Wind chimes?" Garren asked. He glanced at Herbie, who shrugged his wings and winked.

"Yes!" Elise turned toward the window and the cold, bare trees outside. She looked right through Herbie. "But it was only my imagination, wasn't it?"

"Or maybe it was one of those angels from your old neighborhood, laughing because he finally caught up with you."

"I'm sure!" Elise giggled, handing Garren his coat and gloves.

"So am I," Garren said when his back was to her. "So am I."

Elise touched his shoulder, and he turned to face her. Her cheeks were flushed; she seemed suddenly shy. Slowly, she made the sign for "thank you."

"For what?"

Another pause. Then she said simply, "Things."

Chapter

14

"Tonight's the night, isn't it?" Ears asked, setting his lunch tray down and sliding in next to Garren.

Garren nodded and took another bite of his hot dog. "Dad's picking me up right after school," he mumbled between chews.

"A Notre Dame basketball game!" Ears said, smearing mustard up and down his bun. "Think you'll get any autographs?"

Garren slurped the last of his milk. "Could be. We've got box seats. And my dad knows the coach personally."

"Too cool!" Ears licked mustard off his fingers. "So how's it going with the shrink?"

"She's okay."

"And your folks . . . are they . . ."

"They're okay, too." Garren stuffed his napkin into the empty milk carton. "Things are . . . better . . . I think. Mom doesn't cry much anymore—but maybe that's because she doesn't have time to think about it. With all the Christmas shopping, she's at the bookstore a lot. And Dad, well . . . Dad's doing good, I guess."

"Still living at Motel 8?" Ears shoved the last of his hot dog into his mouth.

Garren nodded. He touched his pocket to make sure it

was still there. The Warren Dunes picture. Tonight he would give it to Dad, and he would remember how it used to be, how happy the three of them were. "But I think he might be coming home soon."

The bell blared the end of lunch. Both boys hurried toward the window with their trays.

"Hey, if they pass out free shirts or anything at the game, remember your friends stuck back home!" Ears yelled as they pushed their way into the crowded hall.

"For sure!" Garren waved, heading for his locker.

He was sitting in social studies when the note came. An office aide delivered it to Mr. Hoffer, who pointed out Garren. The girl walked back and laid it on his desk. For an instant Garren stared at the folded piece of paper. Kids usually got notes if they forgot an ortho appointment or something. Once a girl in first hour got one when her grandmother died. What could it be? Slowly he unfolded it and read: "Your father called to say he can't make it tonight. He will call you at home later." That was all. No explanation. No apology. Garren read it again. Then he wadded it up—hard and loud. Mr. Hoffer looked his way. *Go ahead*, Garren thought. *Make my day*. But Mr. Hoffer only went back to lecturing on Indonesia. Shoving his chair back, Garren walked over to the trash can and slammed the crumpled note into it. *Two points*, he thought bitterly. Then, on purpose, he kicked the trash can.

"Temper tantrum over?" Mr. Hoffer stood, lecture notes in hand, staring at Garren.

Garren clenched his fists. *No, I think I'll slam-dunk a few dozen maps, too.* His face felt hot, and he could hear his heart pounding in his ears. *Why? Why did Dad have to cancel out tonight?* He stomped back to his seat and sat down. Mr. Hoffer looked mad, and for an instant Garren thought he was going to send him to the principal's office. But instead he turned to the board and began writing the homework assignment. An assignment Garren decided he wouldn't do.

When school was over, Garren grabbed his coat out of his

locker and headed for the nearest door. He didn't want to see anybody, not even Ears. He'd told Coach he couldn't come to practice because he was going to Notre Dame with his dad—and now he didn't want to have to explain why he wasn't. He didn't even know why he wasn't.

The wind bit into Garren's cheeks as he walked home. Stuffing his bare hands into his pockets, he thought about the note. Where was Dad when he called? What could be more important than a Notre Dame game? What did he mean when he said he'd call "later"? *He probably won't call at all!* Garren thought, tossing an icy snowball at the Ridge Street sign on the corner. Suddenly, Garren felt the wet *smack* of a snowball on his neck. He whirled around. Nothing. "Hey!" he yelled. No one was in sight. Warily, he started toward his house. Another snowball whizzed past his nose. He scooped up a handful of snow and crouched, waiting. *Who's doing this? He's got a pretty good aim whoever he is.* And then he saw her, hiding behind the Deaf Child Area sign. Elise. Running from tree to tree, Garren got close. Then he pelted her on the back.

"Ow!" she screamed, turning to face him. When she saw the two snowballs in his hands, she signed, "You win!" Elise smiled when she saw that Garren understood. She had been teaching him sign so they could communicate when other people were around. Despite his reassurances about her voice, Elise refused to speak in public.

Garren motioned for her to walk with him. "What are you doing home so early?" he asked, dropping the snowballs onto the road.

"No school," she signed. "What are *you* doing home so early?" Then she made the motions of basketball dribbling and shooting.

Garren scuffed at the snow on the sidewalk. His frayed lace was crusted with ice. Elise put her arm on his and they stopped. "My Dad couldn't go," Garren said, facing her. "He . . . he . . ."

They stood in the December grayness, the cold wind shaking the bare trees overhead. "I'm sorry," Elise signed.

"Forget it!" Garren said. "It's no big deal." He gave Elise a quick wave and started up his sidewalk. As he reached for the key inside his jean pocket, he heard the phone ringing. *Bring-ring-ing. Bring-ring-ing.* Dad! His cold hands fumbled with the lock. Just as he pushed open the door, the phone stopped ringing. He stood staring at it for a long time, the silence of the house wrapping itself around him like thick fog. Then, pulling the Warren Dunes picture from his pocket, he sat down on the floor and cried. Really cried.

Garren chewed on the Popsicle stick and pushed the off button on the remote control. He was still hungry. Every channel seemed to be showing food commercials. Thinking he'd be with his dad, Mom hadn't left dinner on the stove. "Not even any decent leftovers," he said aloud, staring into the frosty whiteness of the refrigerator. "Guess it's cheese sandwich time."

Just then the doorbell rang, and Garren jumped. For an instant, he'd thought it was the phone. He clicked on the front porch light and saw Elise, stamping her feet and holding a plate covered with foil.

"Brrr-rrr," she said, hurrying through the open door. "For you." She raised a corner of the foil and the aroma of spaghetti filled the room.

Garren patted his stomach. "Thanks," he said, taking the plate from her.

Elise looked around the room. "Are . . . are you . . . all right?"

Garren nodded. "I'm waiting for my dad to call." He looked toward the phone.

Elise followed his gaze. "Well, I have to go right back anyway." She tapped the foil with her fingernail. "Eat!" she commanded.

"I will," Garren said.

His mouth was full of meatballs when the phone rang. He

stared at it, wanting to answer—but afraid, too. What if it wasn't Dad? What if he had some dumb excuse?

Bring-ring-ing. Bring-ring—

Garren grabbed the receiver. "Hello?" he said, gulping down his last bite of meatball.

"Garren! It's Dad. How you doing?"

How do you think I'm doing? Garren thought. "What happened, Dad? We were supposed to see Notre Dame play tonight!"

"Hey, listen, Son. I'm real sorry about that. You got my message, didn't you?"

"I got it."

"We'll go another time. Maybe even visit the locker room. Would you like that?"

"What happened, Dad?" Garren felt each word form on his tongue before he said it. His own voice sounded odd—older, somehow.

Dad sighed. "A deal, Garren. This great deal that I'd been trying to close for three months. At the last minute the manager said he could see me this afternoon late, that he was ready to buy."

"And that was more important?"

"Look, it's a chain of stores! This could mean big things for me—for all of us."

Us. Who's us?

"We'll take in another game. I swear it, Garren."

Silence.

"I have to go," Garren said.

"Right . . . well . . . take care of yourself." Dad cleared his throat. "I'll see you Sunday. And I'm really sorry, Garren. It was business."

"Sure." Garren said, twisting the phone cord. "I understand."

"Good-bye, Son."

"Bye, Dad."

Even after the click on Dad's end, Garren held onto the phone—the loud drone of the dial tone filling up the empty space between them.

Chapter 15

37 right, 22 left, 4 right. Garren clicked open his locker. Herbie was sitting on the top shelf, leafing through a science book. "Did you know a giraffe and a mouse have the same number of bones in their necks?" he asked.

"What are you doing here?" Garren whispered.

"Waiting to talk to you. Have you asked her yet?"

Garren tossed his math book into the bottom of his locker and reached for his home ec folder. "Not exactly."

"How can you 'not exactly' ask someone to the Christmas dance?"

"Well, Ears is going to ask K.C. to ask Jennifer if she's going to the Christmas party with anyone."

"It took fewer people to storm the walls of Jericho," Herbie sighed.

"I've got to go." Garren slammed the locker and started down the hall.

"You forgot your lab sheets!" Herbie called, his voice echoing from inside the locker. He stuffed the papers through the locker vents.

Garren scanned the halls to make sure no one was looking. "Thanks," he whispered into his locker.

"Ask her!" Herbie yelled back.

"So what'd she say?" Garren asked Ears.

"Who?" Ears said, unwrapping a fresh piece of gum.

"K.C.! About Jennifer!"

"Oh." Ears smiled, chewing his gum thoughtfully. "That." He stopped in front of the drinking fountain. "K.C.'s absent."

"Oh, no! What do I do now—"

"Excuse me, could I get a drink?"

Garren turned. It was Jennifer.

"Uh . . . sure. Here, let me hold it for you." Garren twisted the handle as Jennifer bent over the arc of water. Ears gave him the thumbs-up sign and winked. Garren shook his head.

"I'm finished." Jennifer smiled. Embarrassed, Garren let go of the handle.

"I hear the Christmas party's going to be great!" Ears looked at Garren.

"I've cut out so many paper snowflakes my fingers are frozen." Jennifer laughed.

The three of them stood there. "Oh, my gosh!" Ears said, looking at his bare wrist, "would you look at the time! I've got to get to science. If my Venus flytrap isn't fed on time, she throws dirt all over the room." Then, behind Jennifer's back, he mouthed to Garren, "Now!"

"He's funny." Jennifer giggled.

"Yeah, a barrel of laughs." Garren and Jennifer walked down the hall.

"So, are you going to the Christmas party?" she asked.

"Me? Well . . . maybe. I mean yes. I want to go if . . ."

"If what?"

"Come on kid," Herbie whispered, appearing on Garren's shoulder. "This is your big chance!"

Garren's tongue felt thick and awkward. "If you'll go with me." He stared down at the dusty baseboards.

"Sure!" Jennifer smiled. "That'll be fun."

Garren looked up. "You will? It will? Great!"

"Talk to you later!" she said, disappearing inside the girls' locker room.

"Yeah, later." Garren stood in the middle of the hallway, kids on their way to class swerving around him the way water breaks around a big rock.

"Nice work," Herbie said, his gold teeth glinting.

"She's going with me!" Garren said, laughing. "She's really going with me!"

Three girls stopped and stared at him. Blushing, he ducked his head and headed for class.

"Sharp!" Herbie said, flicking a piece of lint off Garren's dress pants. "And the tie is perfect."

Garren put his foot up on the bed and gave his dress loafers one more swipe with the shoe brush. Then he walked to the full-length mirror at the end of the hall and gave himself the once-over from head to toe. Not bad. He was beginning to really like the way his hair curled over his collar in back. *If only I were a little taller.*

"It's okay." Herbie smiled, reading Garren's thoughts. "Jennifer's shoes are really flat." He reached inside his robe and brought out a perfect white flower. In its very center, a tiny snowflake sparkled. "For Jennifer."

"Wow, thanks!" Garren said. He grabbed his coat from the closet and headed toward his mother's room. "Mom, I'm ready to go."

His mother turned from her makeup mirror and looked at him. For a long time.

"Is . . . is anything wrong?"

She reached for a Kleenex and touched the corners of her eyes. "No, you look wonderful. So grown-up and so much like . . ."

"Like what?" Garren asked.

"Like your father. He wasn't much older than you the first time I saw him."

Garren swallowed. He never knew what to say to Mom anymore. Was that supposed to be a compliment or what?

Stifling a sniffle, she touched her cheekbones with the blush brush and ran the lipstick lightly across her lips. When she stood up and faced Garren, she was smiling. "So, let's go get that lucky lady." Then she saw the white flower. "How lovely! Where did you get it?"

"Persia," Herbie said.

"Uh, a friend got it for me to give to Jennifer. Think she'll like it?"

"I'm absolutely sure of it!" Mom bent down and straightened Garren's tie. "Have a good time, baby."

He stiffened. "Mom, I'm not a baby anymore."

"No," Mom sighed, reaching for her car keys lying on the dresser. "I guess you're not."

Jennifer's parents drove Garren home from the dance. Herbie was waiting inside the door when he got back. "Have a good time, kid?"

Garren grinned. "The best. The disc jockey played all the cool songs. They had this great pink cake with candy cane icing."

"And Jennifer?" Herbie prodded.

"And Jennifer was the prettiest girl there. We danced all the slow dances together." Garren had his foot on the bottom step when he heard the sound of TV coming from the family room. "Mom?"

Herbie nodded. "She's watching the late show—and waiting for you."

Garren slipped out of his dress shoes and loosened his tie. The only light in the family room was the Christmas tree. It stood in front of the bow window, where it had stood every year since Garren could remember. Same ornaments. Same lights. Same tinsel. *Too bad a few other things aren't the same.* "Hi, Mom."

Garren's mom looked up. "Have a good time?"

"Sure."

"And your . . . date . . . did she enjoy the dance?"

Garren shrugged. "I guess so. What are you watching?"

Mother smiled. "A golden oldie. *It's a Wonderful Life* with Jimmy Stewart. I can't tell you how many times I've seen it—but every Christmas I watch it again. It's almost over. Come watch the end with me." She patted the couch beside her.

Garren sat down next to his mom. She put her arm around him, and he leaned against her. On the screen, a man and his family were gathered in front of a Christmas tree. All the man's neighbors and friends were there, too. They were giving him money. Some of them were laughing; some of them were crying. Mom was doing both. The movie ended with a big crescendo and a close-up of the family—father, mother, children.

A real family, Garren thought as THE END came across the screen. Would they ever be a real family again? Were all the happy endings reserved for old movies—or were there a few left over for real life?

Chapter

16

"Ah, my favorite time of year!" Herbie said, circling the Christmas tree and humming "Hark the Herald Angels Sing" along with the radio.

Garren finished putting out the nativity set—shepherds, sheep, wise men, angel. Mary, Joseph, Jesus. *Mother, father, child—a real family*, Garren thought. *Just like we were last Christmas.*

"Deck the halls with boughs of holly. . . ." Herbie danced around the fake yellow angel on top of the tree. "Hey, where'd you get this ugly thing anyway?" he asked, playfully jabbing its plastic face.

"Hey, watch it!" Garren said, grabbing the angel just as it tumbled from the branch.

"Oh, sorry." Herbie helped Garren prop the angel back into place and straightened a few of the bright bulbs.

"Some of these ornaments are really special!" Gently, Garren touched his favorite—a shiny blue ball.

"And old," Herbie said, fluttering down and landing on the arm of the couch.

"I made this when I was in kindergarten," Garren said, touching the pom-pom snowman. "And this matchstick nativity we made in Sunday school. I got more glue on me than I did on the matches!"

"Ornaments come in all shapes and sizes, don't they?"

"Sure."

"Kind of like people."

Garren thought for a minute. "I guess so."

"I mean, there's Elise and Ears, and Jennifer and K.C., and Mr. Hoffer—"

"Please!" Garren groaned. "I'm on vacation! I don't even want to think about school."

"You know, kid, families can be as different as people."

Garren looked at Herbie. A shaft of winter sun shone through the window, creating a glistening whiteness around him. "You're not going to start preaching, are you, Herbie?"

"No, no! I was just thinking aloud . . . about families. Elise and her father are a family. Ears and his four sisters and their parents are a family. When old Mr. Norris lived next door with his six cats, they were a family."

"So what?" Garren said, a touch of resentment in his voice.

"So—you're still part of a family this Christmas. You've still got two parents who love you very much."

"Yeah, they just can't stand to be in the same room together!" Garren picked up a package with his name on it and shook it.

"Socks," Herbie said.

Garren stopped shaking the gift. "You know what's in every one of these, don't you?"

"Of course."

"So . . . am I going to get what I asked for?"

"The weight set?"

Garren nodded.

"My lips are sealed." Herbie pretended to zip his mouth.

"Well, unseal them and tell me!"

Herbie shook his head.

"At least give me a hint. What are my chances of getting it? Better than fifty percent?"

Herbie laughed, and in a whirl of angel dust and a tinkle of wind chimes, disappeared.

"Thanks for nothing!" Garren yelled into midair.

The hall clock struck one. Garren still had an hour before Dad picked him up. He decided to give Ears a call. But when he picked up the phone, he heard his mom's voice. She was on the extension in her bedroom. And she was talking to— Dad!

"But they're so expensive!" she said.

"I know, but it's the only thing he asked for, really." Dad sounded tired.

"You still haven't paid for his dentist appointment last month."

"I'll get around to it. It's Christmas, for pete's sake. Forget about the bills and let's get Garren what he wants."

"Forget about the bills? That's easy for you to say. You don't have the phone company and the gas company and the electric company sending you threatening notes if their checks are a few days late."

Dad sighed. "What would *you* suggest we get him?"

"I don't know. Clothes are always good. And we have some excellent new books down at the store—"

"No!" Dad said, his voice taking on the loud anger Garren remembered from his parents' old fights. "When I was a kid, all I ever got for Christmas was clothes. I want Garren to have that weight set. I'll put it on my credit card."

Garren's mother was quiet for a moment. "You can't buy him, you know."

"What are you talking about?"

"I'm talking about bribing him with expensive gifts. With junk food and video games every time you see him. With promises of locker room visits and pro autographs."

"Bribes! Can't a father show his son a good time if he wants? If you had your way, he'd be wearing an apron and—"

Softly, Garren laid the receiver back in place. His stomach felt like he'd swallowed a fast ball. Why did they have to argue all the time? And about him?

Someone on the radio was singing "Silent Night." "All is

calm, all is bright," the voice crooned. *Not around here*, Garren thought, shaking another present. *Not around here!*

The tree seemed to stretch up forever, touching the night sky. "Wow," Garren said, leaning his head back and looking up at the lights. "Must have taken a helicopter to hang that star on top!"

Dad laughed. "Or at least a boom truck." They stood in Daley Plaza, the hustle and bustle of Chicago moving around them. Garren liked the city best at night, especially during the holiday season when every street lamp boasted red bows and garland. "Get enough pizza?" Dad asked.

"Plenty!" Gino's made the best pizza in Chicago. Maybe the world.

Together they began walking down Randolph toward State Street, pausing to look in decorated windows at animated elves and reindeer, at plump Santas and delicate angels. Sounds of Christmas carols came from the next block, where three people in Salvation Army uniforms were playing instruments. A young girl about Garren's age was ringing a bell beside a red bucket. Reaching into his pocket, Dad grabbed a handful of change and gave it to Garren. "'Tis the season." He smiled, nodding toward the group. Garren went over and dumped the change down the slit in the top of the bucket. It clanked onto the pile of money inside.

"God bless you," the girl said.

Garren smiled. "You, too."

They were halfway to their car when it started snowing. Thick flakes landed on Dad's overcoat like tiny UFOs. While they walked, Garren kept remembering what the Salvation Army girl had said. "God bless you." He'd been thinking about God a lot lately. Like how powerful everybody said he was. And how much he was supposed to love you. About how he could make blind people see and lame people walk and stuff like that. In his sermon last Sunday, Pastor had talked about miracles, about how God could do anything.

Then why doesn't he get Mom and Dad to stop fighting? Why doesn't he put an end to this stupid separation? Maybe Herbie would know.

Dad cleared his throat as they started down the steps into the parking garage. "I . . . I've got something I've been meaning to tell you." Garren looked up. His dad's face was serious. "I'm moving out of Motel 8."

Garren's breath seemed to freeze inside him. Moving? Back home? He couldn't bring himself to ask it.

"My friend Jake Metts—you remember Jake, don't you? He stopped by the house a few times to drop off shoe samples. Well, he has a two-bedroom apartment. He's on the road most of the time, anyway." Dad unlocked Garren's door and stood there, fingering his key ring. "So I'm going to stay with him until . . ."

Until what? Garren stomped his feet, sending little avalanches of white onto the concrete floor.

"I'm going to stay with him for a while." Dad walked around to his side. Garren got in and slammed the door. He could feel Dad looking at him as he started the car, waiting for him to say something. What was there to say?

Slowly, they drove through the low-ceilinged underground garage, inching their way toward the surface. Jake. Garren couldn't remember ever meeting anyone named Jake. But by the time they'd maneuvered through traffic and swung onto the Indiana tollway, Garren had made up his mind. He didn't like Jake. Not one little bit.

Chapter 17

"What's in it?" Garren held the envelope his mother had given him.

"A surprise. A surprise Christmas gift," she said, beaming.

He pulled open the flap. Inside was a ticket. A ticket to what? Garren took it out and began reading, "Delta Airlines, Flight 742—"

"It's from your grandparents. Florida! I've got one, too. We're going to Florida!" Mom clapped her hands. She danced around the room. "I've been dying to tell you. I've known for almost a month. That's why I've been working so much overtime. I've got all next week off! No cash registers or returns or shelves to restock. Just sand and sun and sea shells."

Garren looked outside. Fresh snow had fallen during the night, perfect for sledding and fort-building and snowball fights. Maybe even skiing at the Pines if Ears's dad would take them. Florida? At Christmas? "What about Dad?"

Mother stood still and looked at Garren. "What about him?"

"Well . . . is he . . ."

"He's certainly not coming with us! These tickets are a gift from my parents so you and I can visit them."

"But what will he do on Christmas?"

"I'm sure I have no idea. He and Jake probably have something planned," Mom said, an icy tone coming into her voice. "But he's coming over later to bring your Christmas present. You can ask him then."

Christmas present . . . the weight set?

"In the meantime," Mom said, her enthusiasm returning, "I have some last-minute shopping to do. And *you* better get packing. We leave tomorrow! We'll open the presents under the tree tonight."

Garren trudged up to his bedroom. At least he'd already wrapped the new sweatshirt he'd bought Mom. Of course, she probably wouldn't need it in Florida.

"Are you coming with us?" Garren asked Herbie.

"Wouldn't miss it!" Herbie tossed Garren's sunglasses into the suitcase.

"You'll like my grandma. She makes the best walnut fudge. And Grandpa tells knock-knock jokes all the time," Garren laughed, his mood brightening. He finished packing his socks and shorts. "I always love going to see them. They live in this trailer court that's only a few blocks from the beach. But . . . I don't know . . . I've never been away from home at Christmas before." Garren clicked the suitcase shut.

"And you're worried about your dad."

"What's he supposed to do on Christmas?" Garren walked to his dresser and picked up a small package. Inside was the gold Cross pen he'd bought at the office supply store. "I was going to give this to him then."

"Give it to him now," Herbie said, just as Dad's car pulled into the driveway.

"Merry Christmas!" Dad shouted when Garren opened the door. His dress shoes were all covered with snow, and he knocked them together before he came inside. He lifted a big—really big—present over the threshold. "Santa wanted me to drop this off. He's running behind schedule and asked me to help him out." He dragged Garren's gift over to the couch before taking off his coat.

It was an old joke between them. Dad as Santa's helper. It

had started the Christmas Garren was six and had found his dad putting together the race track he'd wanted.

"What a coincidence," Garren said, reaching for Dad's package. "He asked me to give this to you."

Dad looked surprised, then pleased. "Why, that old geezer is getting lazy! Shall I open it now?"

Garren thought about Christmas morning. About Dad at Jake's. "If you want to, or you might want to . . . you know . . . wait."

Dad held the box, touching the red stick-on bow. "I think I'll wait," he said, setting it on top of his coat. He looked around the room. "Tree looks nice."

"Same as always." Garren shrugged.

Dad sat down. "I guess so."

"You . . . uh . . . know about Florida?"

Dad crossed his legs and wiped at a scuff mark on his shoe. "I know." Then, looking up at Garren, he smiled. "Should be a lot of fun! While us working stiffs are up here digging out of snowdrifts you'll be catching a few rays."

"Yeah, a lot of fun." *If it's going to be so much fun, why do I sound like I'm going to the dentist instead of on vacation?*

"Present time!" Dad said, maneuvering the awkward package toward Garren. "This is from both of us . . . your mom and me."

Garren stared at it, remembering the phone conversation. Was Mom still mad? Then, in a rush of excitement, he began ripping at the paper. The weight set! Steel barbell bar with revolving sleeve, outside collars, inside collars, dumbbells. Everything! "Thanks, Dad! Thanks a lot!"

Dad punched his arm. "Those biceps should get a real workout with these."

"For sure! Let's put them together."

Dad glanced at his watch. "Better hold off on that, sport."

A familiar sadness began to creep up inside Garren. "Got an appointment or something?" he asked, running his finger around the heavy gray collars.

"Have to sell a lot of shoes to pay for this!" Dad joked,

reaching for his coat. He tucked Garren's gift in his inside pocket. "First thing when you get back from Florida—we'll put her together then."

They stood at the door, an awkward silence between them.

"Thanks for the weight set."

"I'll tell Santa you said that." Dad's smile faded a bit. "Have a good trip. Talk to you when you get back." Then, quickly, Dad gave Garren a one-armed hug.

Garren pressed his forehead against the cold glass and watched Dad pull away from the curb. Only then did he realize he'd forgotten to ask what he would do—just him and Jake—on Christmas Day.

Chapter

18

"So, how was your Christmas vacation?" Garren and Ears stood in line, waiting their turns to shoot free throws.

"Okay—I missed the snow, though. All it did in Florida was rain." Garren looked down at his white legs. "I didn't get any tan at all."

Ears stepped forward, pushing his toes against the line. Making a big circle with the ball, he tossed it up. It arced higher and higher, hit the rim, and bounced off. He stood to one side and tossed the rebound to Garren. "No, but I hear you got something else!"

"The weight set." Garren grinned, tossing the ball through the hoop with a solid *swoosh*. "It's great! Dad came over last night and we put it together. Can't wait to start pumping iron!" They took their places at the end of the line. "What'd you get?"

"A bunch of tapes, some new stickers for my board, clothes. Couple of posters. Grandma got me a year's subscription to *Skater* magazine. And my sisters went in together and filled my stocking with batteries for my tape player."

Coach Cannon blew the whistle. "Last man in line, collect those balls! Rest of you hit the showers—and no horsing around in the locker room!" He watched each boy file past.

"Hey, Gillum," he said when Garren tossed the last ball into the big bag, "did Santa bring you anything good for Christmas?"

"You bet!" Garren said, smiling. "A weight set!"

Coach nodded his approval. "Good, good. But I was kind of hoping he'd bring you something else."

"Like what?"

"A pair of scissors!" Coach said, turning his back on Garren and dragging the bag of balls into the storage room.

Garren tried to swallow the anger he felt churning inside him. He touched his hair. What was wrong with it? Before each wrestling meet he'd been clipping it just a little—just enough to get by. "One of these days—"

"Forget it," Ears said, grabbing Garren's arm and steering him toward the locker room.

All morning long it snowed, until the parking lot was white and drifts hugged the tires on the teachers' cars. Everywhere there were whispers of "Think we'll get to go home early?" Rumors about roads drifting shut circulated among students. Finally, just after lunch, the announcement came. Early dismissal!

Garren kicked his way through the fresh snow on the sidewalks. Everywhere was a blinding whiteness—and still the flakes were falling. By the time he reached Ridge Street, Garren was a moving mountain of frozen crystals. He wondered if Elise would be home. She would love this. As Garren glanced in the direction of his house, a splash of color caught his eye. Someone was on his front porch— someone wearing a bright red cape. Who could it be? Whoever she was, she was shaking the door handle to make sure it was locked. A burglar? For an instant Garren stopped, unsure of what to do.

Suddenly the lady turned to face him. Her round, lipsticked mouth broke into a smile. "You look like the Abominable Snowman," she laughed, coming down the walk toward him.

"This is my house," Garren said.

She paused with the key in her hand. "It is? Well, and a fine house it is, too! Bedrooms are a bit small and the kitchen could stand a tad of remodeling. But the basement is good and dry and the attic well-insulated." She made a few notes on the clipboard she was carrying, shielding her writings from the snow. "I'm sure it will sell quickly."

"Sell?"

She looked at him, her mouth pulled into the shape of a Cheerio. "Oooh, I guess no one told you."

"Told me what?" Inside his wet shoes, Garren wiggled his toes, trying to shake off the cold that gripped his insides.

The lady pulled a business card from her pocket. "Harley Snyder Real Estate. Your mother asked me to come by and appraise the house."

Real estate? Appraise? "Why?" It was the only word Garren could make his tongue form.

"Why don't you take that up with her?" the lady said, handing Garren the key and patting his shoulder. Then, holding onto the hood of a big blue Lincoln parked in front of Elise's, she inched her way around the car and into the driver's seat. After several spins, she pulled away from the curb.

Garren unlocked the door and stepped inside. The house smelled of lemons and pine. *Cleaning day.* What did that lady mean by "sell quickly"? As Garren headed for his room he took the steps two at a time, sending showers of melting snow into the carpet. *Our house isn't for sale! Or is it?* He'd ask Mom when she got home from work. The minute she got home from work.

Mom was late. Garren paced back and forth in the family room, looking first at the clock and then out the window. The snow had finally stopped, but the wind was picking up, tossing white swirls onto deepening drifts. What if something had happened to her? Garren thought about Elise's mother, about the car accident. What if Mom were . . .

The familiar whirr of the electric garage door opener signaled Mom's safe arrival. Garren sighed with relief. He stood facing the door, waiting. Mom pushed it open, shaking the snow from her hat and bending over to unzip her boots. She sensed Garren's presence and looked up. "Whoo! Can you believe this? The joys of winter in northwest Indiana! I heard on the radio that you got out of school early." She came inside and sank into the couch. She wiggled her toes and closed her eyes. "What a drive! I'd never have made it if I hadn't followed that snowplow."

Garren couldn't wait any longer. "Is our house for sale?"

Mom opened her eyes. "Of course not! What on earth—"

She saw the Harley Snyder Real Estate card on the coffee table. "You met the realtor?" Garren nodded. "I was going to tell you."

"When? Just before the moving van arrived?" Garren's voice got louder with each word.

"It was just an appraisal, baby. Just so I'd know how much this place was worth. If things don't work out between your dad and me—"

"How *can* they work out if you plan for them not to?" Garren was yelling now. "You want a divorce, don't you?"

Mom looked as though she had been slapped. "No. I don't."

Garren stared at her, at the silent tears splashing onto her sweater. How many tears had she cried? A thousand? A million? He tried to take a deep breath, but his insides were being squeezed, somehow. He was mad and sorry at the same time.

"But I don't want things the way they were before your father left, either." There was a calm quietness to her voice that scared Garren. "I have to have a life with some peace, some kind of order. Can you understand that?"

Garren sat down beside her. He could understand that. But couldn't she understand that this was the only home he'd ever known? That he wanted—needed—two parents?

"I don't want to sell the house." She put her arm around him, running her finger around his shoulder blade in soft circles, the way she used to do when he was little and couldn't fall asleep. "I just need to know how much equity we have. I need to know what my assets are, how much money we *have* compared to how much we *owe*. Maybe we won't have to sell. Maybe we'll live here until I'm an old woman with white hair and you're the father of triplets." She tried to laugh.

Maybe we won't sell the house. Maybe I'll be "Most Valuable Wrestler." Maybe Dad will come back home.

Maybe. It was becoming the biggest word in Garren's vocabulary.

Chapter

19

The mats swarmed with wrestlers practicing takedowns and pins. Garren sat to one side, scanning the gym for his competition. No Lynchburg. Some faces he recognized; others were new. This was a big invitational tournament, and lots of schools had brought teams. He'd have to wrestle five, maybe six times before it was all over. Garren unscrewed the lid on his Gatorade and took a slow swallow. It was going to be a long day.

"The half! Work the half! You're wrestling like an old woman!" The veins in Coach's neck stood out like blue lines on a map. Mosier was sweating. He strained against his opponent, struggling to his feet. An escape! "Now, work it!" Mosier's muscles strained as he tried for a four-point move. Up, up, over! The referee held up four fingers. Mosier was ahead by one! "Thirty-five seconds!" Coach screamed. Mosier's move stalled, and the ref brought both boys back to the center of the mat. A blast of his whistle, and the match began again. In a flash, Mosier's opponent shot. Take down! Now Mosier was behind by one. "Point! Point!" Coach yelled, his voice gravelly and desperate. But the towel sailed across the mat, signaling the end of the round. Head down, Mosier walked back to the center of the mat and watched as the ref raised the hand of his opponent. "Tough break,"

Coach said, slapping Mosier's behind. "Got to be quicker. Get a bigger lead in the first round before you tire out." Mosier nodded and squeezed his water bottle, letting the lukewarm stream drizzle down his throat.

Garren had watched it all from staging, where he sat waiting to be paired with his next competitor. Mosier had lost—and Coach had counted on him to win. Hinkle Creek was in first place by only a few points. So far Garren had been winning. Now it would be even more important to get those points for his team. "Gillum!" the man yelled, waving a bout sheet.

"Here!" Garren stood up.

"Swayze." A stocky boy Garren had never seen before also stepped forward. He looked tough. A sneer curled his lip as he sized up Garren. "Mat 8," the man said, handing Garren the sheet and motioning them toward the far end of the gym.

Silently the two boys stood, waiting their turn. Swayze jogged in place. Garren pulled off his sweatshirt and began doing windmills with his arms, warming up his muscles for the match. *Win! Pin! Win! Pin!* Garren chanted it inside his head until the noise of the gym melted into the rhythm. *Win! Pin!* Suddenly, he was on deck. And then the ref was calling his name. Garren walked to the middle of the mat and faced Swayze. As always, the ref checked their nails and ran his hands across their shoulders and arms, making sure the boys were dry. Satisfied, he put his whistle in his mouth and was about to start the match. Then he paused. He looked at Garren for a long time. Slowly, he took his whistle out of his mouth and let it hang from its black cord. Looking toward the officials at the scoring table, he yelled. "Hair is too long." He touched Garren's shoulder with his sweaty hand. "Ten minutes to correct the situation, then he forfeits. Next match!" He waved Gillum and Swayze off the mat.

Garren felt numb. Forfeit? He'd never forfeited in his life! Not even the time his nose was busted up so badly the medics thought it was broken. But even if he wanted to, how could he get a haircut in the next ten minutes? And that's when he saw Coach, standing at the edge of the mat holding the first-aid kit.

"It's up to you, Gillum," Coach said when he got closer. "We need this win. *You* need this win." He opened the first-aid kit and took out a small pair of scissors. Their *snip-snip* sounded above the noise in the gym. Garren touched his hair. First-aid scissors? With Coach using them? Not a chance!

Without speaking, Garren walked past Coach and to the drinking fountain at the other end of the gym. He looked at the clock, remembering the ref's words. *Ten minutes to correct.* He had eight minutes left. He drank and drank. When he finally finished, he raised up and came face to face with Swayze. The smirk was a full-faced grin now. "Nice match," he said, flicking the back of Garren's hair. "You were even easier than I thought!" He laughed as he pushed Garren aside and bent to get a drink.

Six minutes left.

It's my hair, Garren thought. *No one can make me cut it.*

"True, kid." It was Herbie, hovering just overhead. "You can choose not to cut your hair; you can choose to win this tournament for Hinkle Creek. But you can't choose to do both."

"Why not?" Garren said, his voice blending with the yelling in the gym. "I'm just as good a wrestler with long hair!"

"But you'll never get the chance to show Swayze—and your own team—that."

"It's a dumb rule!" Garren yelled just as the hand on the clock moved. Five minutes. He closed his eyes and saw—for the thousandth time—Mom and Dad at the awards banquet. Together.

Then suddenly he was pushing through the crowd, calling Coach's name. He still stood at the edge of Mat 8, waiting. "Cut it!" Garren said, turning his back and biting his lip. And with a quick *snip-snip-snip*, several long pieces of hair fell to the floor. Garren stepped over them, anger and determination pumping through him. "Ready to wrestle!" he yelled to the ref. And he really was.

Everyone was rowdy on the way home. The bus walls seemed to shake with the yelling and singing, with the laughter and joking. They had won. Hinkle Creek had defeated a dozen other schools and come away with the trophy. "Ice cream—my treat!" Coach shouted as the bus turned into the parking lot of the Dairy Freeze. The boys piled out, shoving to be first in line. All except Garren. He sat in his seat, his sweatshirt hood pulled close around his face. Coach was about to follow the team when he noticed him. "That was quite a match, Gillum," he said from the front of the bus. "You wrestled like a madman!"

Garren pulled his hood down even further. He could feel the bluntness of his freshly cut hair, the stubbiness left by the whacks of those first-aid scissors. He'd have to get a real cut when he got home.

"Come on," Coach said, a strange tenderness in his voice. "A good dose of hot fudge will make you feel better." But still Garren sat in silence. With a shake of his head, Coach stepped off the bus.

All at once the whole bus echoed with the pounding of dozens of fists outside. "Gillum, Gillum, Gillum!" the boys were shouting. "Yea, Gillum!" The racket got even louder. "Gillum, Gillum, Gillum!"

A slow smile worked its way across Garren's face. He had won. And because of that, so had the team. True, it had cost him. Garren shook the sweatshirt hood off his head and touched the fuzzy brittleness along his neck. But he was one win closer to undefeated, one step nearer to getting Mom and Dad back together again. *Besides*, he thought, pushing open the bus door, *I can always let it grow—once things get back to normal at home.*

Chapter

20

"What do you mean you're not going to tell her?" Elise tossed another handful of popcorn into her mouth.

"I just won't tell her, that's all."

"What about the 'parent's signature' on the bottom?"

Garren fingered his report card, staring at the two red Fs sitting squarely on the lines after *Home Ec* and *Science*. "I'll sign it myself."

Elise's eyes widened. "You're going to forge your mother's name? You could get in big trouble!"

"No more trouble than I'll get in if she sees these grades!" Garren walked over to the fireplace and poked at the logs with a long stick. Over and over he jabbed them until they crumbled into piles of bright embers. Then he turned back to Elise. "See, I've always made good grades. Great grades. Every grading period Mom cuts out the Honor Roll from the paper. She underlines my name in red and then pastes it into a scrap book." Sighing, Garren reached for some popcorn. "But this semester . . . well, I don't know what happened. I forget to do homework. My mind always seems about a million miles away from where it's supposed to be." He shook his head. "Mom'll kill me if she finds out I failed two subjects."

Elise touched his arm. "She'll have to find out sooner or later."

"Later! Much later! Maybe by then my grades'll be up and she won't be so mad." Garren pulled a canceled check from his pocket. "I got this out of her desk so I could practice her signature. I think I can get her first name, but I keep having trouble with the 'Gillum' part. She writes so fancy!"

Elise bent her head close to Garren's, studying the crumpled piece of paper he spread out on the coffee table. Over and over he had written "Rachel Gillum," trying to imitate the round, bold writing of his mother. But every signature looked like what it was—a forgery.

"This is never going to work," Elise said.

Garren knew she was right. He had wasted half a dozen sheets of paper practicing his mother's signature, and he was no closer to being able to copy it than he was before.

"You write like a boy—squinchy little letters and sloppy capitals. Your mother's been signing your report cards for years. They'll know for sure!"

Garren wadded up his practice paper. He hadn't thought of that. The school must have about forty dozen things with Mom's signature on them—report cards and permission slips and book rentals. They'd be sure to check the handwriting. She'd always signed everything. And then it hit him. Dad. Dad had never signed anything! He grinned. "I've got it!"

Elise frowned. "Got what?"

"The solution to my problem! Sure, I write like a boy— but so does Dad. I'll put *his* name on the report card. He's a parent—and the school will never know he didn't write it himself!"

"I don't think that's such a good idea . . ."

But Garren wasn't listening. He already had his coat half-zipped and was heading toward the door.

The next day at school, Garren couldn't find his report card. He looked all through his locker. Again. He shook each book, shuffled through loose papers, checked coat pockets.

106

Nothing. The warning bell sounded. One more tardy and he'd have to serve detention! *Where is it? I know I brought it!* Just as he was about to slam his locker shut, a glint of gold caught his eye. Herbie. Of course! He swung open the door. There Herbie was, sitting on the report card. "Give it to me," Garren said.

"Look, kid, getting bad grades is bad enough. But dishonesty—"

"Give it to me!" he hissed. Kids hurried past Garren heading for homeroom. He leaned into his locker and whispered, "Just butt out! If you'd wanted to help, you could have turned those Fs into Bs. But you didn't, so now don't give me any of your holy advice!" Grabbing the report card, Garren slammed the locker shut with a loud *whang*.

For two days Garren waited, worrying that someone would know. Then, when no phone calls came for Mom, when no notes were sent down from the office, he began to relax. He had done it. Herbie hadn't mentioned the report card affair since that day at school, and neither had Garren. The incident was like a cold barricade between them. Once or twice Garren had wanted to explain, but what could Herbie know about parents? About how they always expected you to be perfect?

They were eating at Gelessomo's when Mom brought it up. "Isn't it about time for report cards?" she said, reaching for another slice of pizza.

Garren almost gagged on his pepperoni. He struggled to swallow his mouthful of food and then took a long, slow drink of his cola. He studied Mom's face. Did she know? Was she fishing for facts, giving him a chance to confess? Or was it just a simple question? "Uh . . . report cards . . . yeah, I guess it must be about time."

Mom wiped her mouth with the red-and-white checkered napkin. "In fact, I thought first semester ended sometime in January. Today's February first."

"Boy, winter sure is flying past!" Garren said, picking mushrooms off his pizza. "Soon spring'll be here. You going to plant any new flowers this spring?" He knew he was talking too fast, but he had to get Mom's mind on something besides report cards. "I like those big pink tulips you planted last year."

"Those were peonies."

"Peonies." Garren pushed his chair back. "Great meal, huh, Mom? Better get home now. Lots of homework—"

"Not so fast, young man." Garren knew that tone of voice. It was the same tone TV cops used when they said "Freeze!" to fleeing criminals.

Even pizza couldn't cover up the sour taste in Garren's mouth as he told Mom about the forgery.

"So how long you grounded for?" Ears asked.

"A whole month. Mom's going to check my homework every night. And she's coming to talk to my home ec and science teachers."

"Tough." They cut across the snow-covered baseball diamond and climbed the drifts at the edge of the school parking lot. The first bell rang just as the boys pushed open the door. A rush of warm air brushed against their tingling cheeks.

"Later!" Ears yelled, sliding his earphones into place and disappearing into the crowd.

When Garren opened his locker, Herbie was waiting for him.

"Hi, kid."

Garren hung up his coat and reached for his spiral notebook. "Hi."

"Don't forget your colored pencils for social studies."

Garren reached into his coat pocket and took out the box. He stared at the pencils' colorful points. Finally he looked up at Herbie. "Go on, say it!"

Herbie scratched his head through his halo. "Say what?"

"'I told you so!' Go ahead and say it! You told me not to sign my own report card, not to keep it from Mom. It was a dumb thing to do. You must be dying to say 'I told you so!'"

"As a matter of fact, I never say that."

"Never?"

"Part of the angel oath," Herbie said, raising his right hand and wiggling his thumb. "We never say . . . those words."

"The angel oath?"

"It's the clause right after the one that says everybody deserves a fresh start." Herbie chuckled, clicking the locker door shut.

A fresh start, Garren thought as he headed for class. *That's what Mom and Dad need, too.* All he had to do was make them realize it. Somehow . . .

Chapter 21

Garren touched his back pocket to make sure the money was still there. A ten-dollar bill he'd gotten for shoveling walks at the apartment complex. He was going to buy valentines for his friends. Not the cartoon type in the big bag, but real cards he'd pick out one by one. But who to buy for? Jennifer. Elise. Maybe Ears. What about Mom? Dad always sent her a big card. Sometimes it was serious, all about love and stuff like that. Other years it was funny. But Garren was almost sure there would be no valentine from Dad this year.

"What this guy needs is a new robe and a decent set of wings!" Herbie flicked the cardboard cutout of Cupid hanging by a thread over the card display at the drugstore. It spun around and around and around.

"Wow! Check out all these valentines!" Garren looked down the long rows. Some were frilly and pink. A few had Snoopy or Garfield on them. Still others were cut in the shape of huge hearts. Garren reached for one close by and began reading.

"This one's clever," Herbie said, pulling a card from the top shelf and taking it to Garren. A lady at the other end stared, her eyes following the drifting card—a look of horror and disbelief on her face.

"Herbie!" Garren whispered, grabbing the floating valentine.

"Sorry," Herbie said, a sheepish grin tugging at the corners of his mouth.

Still staring, the lady backed away from the card counter, cleaning her glasses with a crumpled tissue she dug from her purse.

Finally, the choices were made. There was a funny one for Jennifer. The outside said: "Happy Valentine's Day to one of the cutest people in the world." The inside said: "From the other one." Garren found one with a skateboard on it for Ears. And for Elise there was a serious card, with sparkley hearts and snowflakes that said "To My Friend." Garren read all the "For Mother" greetings, but nothing seemed quite right. He stopped in front of the "Dad" ones—cards with fishing poles baited with hearts and old-fashioned cars with heart-shaped hubcaps. Would Dad want a valentine? Or would he think it was kid stuff? Where would he put it? Garren tried to imagine Dad's room. Briefcase and order forms and shoe samples—and all Jake's stuff piled everywhere. At the very bottom of the shelf, a card caught his eye. It was done in bright colors and had all kinds of sports equipment on its cover—basketballs and tennis rackets, running shoes and soccer balls. Inside it said: "Happy Valentine's Day to a real winner!" Garren stuffed it into his stack of cards. Then, after a bit of mental addition to make sure he had enough money, he picked up two tiny heart-shaped boxes of chocolates and headed for the checkout.

Mom was working late, but the smell of chili simmering in the crockpot filled the house. Garren tossed his coat on the couch and sat down once again to look at his cards. He'd have to get Dad's in the mail tomorrow. He took a pen from his book bag and signed the others. He taped one of the boxes of chocolates on top of Jennifer's card. The other box he set in the middle of the coffee table for Mom.

He was ladling up his second bowl of chili when the doorbell rang. Garren looked out the kitchen window and saw a Shady Lawn Florist truck parked at the curb. Outside the door a man was stamping his feet in the snow, holding a long white box tied with red ribbons. Flowers. Garren opened the door.

"Flowers for Rachel Gillum," the man said, shivering. "Sign here." Garren took the pen and wrote his name on the black line. The delivery man thrust the box into Garren's arms and ran down the sidewalk toward his truck.

Flowers! Garren stepped inside and nudged the door shut with his hip. Dad had come through after all! Garren wanted to open them, to take just a peek at the card, but he knew he shouldn't. Besides, he'd never get all those ribbons tied back just right. *Won't Mom be surprised?* Garren thought. He imagined her tired face breaking into a smile when she saw the box. He could hear her say, as she buried her face in their scent, "That sly fox! He shouldn't have." Then she'd call Dad to thank him. He'd suggest they meet somewhere for coffee. And then . . .

The doorbell rang again. This time it was Elise.

"Hi!" Garren said, opening the door wide enough for her to scamper inside. She held a foil-covered plate in her mittened hands.

"Brrr!" she said, letting her lips shudder like a horse's. "It's cold!" She handed Garren the plate and, taking off her mittens, signed, "Happy Valentine's Day." She had been teaching Garren the gestures for all the holiday greetings.

"Merry Christmas to you, too," he laughed. She swatted him with her mitten. He pulled back the foil. It was a heart-shaped cake with pink icing and a border of tiny red-hot hearts.

"I made it myself."

"I'll eat it anyway." This time he ducked before the mitten struck. "I've got something for you, too." He turned away and reached for the card. He handed it to her and then signed, perfectly, "Happy Valentine's Day."

Elise laughed. She was turning to go when she saw the

box. Her green eyes were filled with curiosity as she looked toward Garren.

"They came for Mom just a few minutes ago."

"Ooh, I bet they're roses!" Elise crooned.

"Yeah, Mom will be real surprised. Dad never did anything like this before."

"How do you know they're from your father?"

"Of course they're from my father! Who else do you think . . ." But Garren stopped. He'd just assumed they were from Dad. He hadn't thought that someone else might be sending his mother flowers. It was a dumb thought. "They're from my dad. I know they are."

Elise shrugged. "Okay, sure." She pulled on her mittens and picked up her card.

"Happy Valentine's Day." Garren forced a smile. "Thanks for the cake."

"Enjoy!" She waved the card. "And thanks!"

When Elise had gone, Garren went back to his chili. It was cold. He dumped it down the disposal and cut a piece of the cake. *How do you know they're from your father?* The question rattled in his head like an unsolved riddle. Admittedly, it wasn't like Dad to send flowers. Especially the expensive kind that come boxed and bowed. But ladies didn't send other ladies those kinds of flowers, either. Which only left . . . Garren shoved a hunk of icing in his mouth. No. They were from Dad. That was that. Still, he wished Mom would get home soon so they could read the card. And be sure.

"Garren! Garren, I'm home!"

Garren had just stepped out of the shower when he heard his mother's voice in the hallway. He dried off quickly, then knotted the big towel around his waist and opened the bathroom door. She was holding a huge bouquet of roses, cradling them so their long stems ended gracefully in the palm of her hand. She looked like Miss America.

"Aren't they beautiful?" She smiled. "And so fragrant! Smell." She leaned the bouquet toward Garren. He took a whiff. "I haven't had flowers like this since I was a teenager."

Garren stood there, his hair dripping on his shoulders, waiting for her to mention Dad.

"I can't imagine what they cost! Better get them in water before they wilt." She turned to go downstairs.

Garren swallowed hard and then spoke. "Yeah, Dad would hate it if you let them wilt."

She stopped, her back to Garren. Slowly she turned around. "They're not from your father, baby."

I didn't hear that, Garren thought.

"They're from Frank. . . ."

Garren just stared at his mother.

"He comes into the bookstore a lot. Wants to be a writer. He's working on his first novel. . . ."

Garren shut his eyes, trying to shut out his mother's voice, too. Frank? No, the flowers were from Dad! Any minute now she'd laugh and say she was just kidding about Frank. She'd show him the card, written in Dad's squiggly handwriting.

But she didn't show him the card, and when Garren opened his eyes, his mother was walking down the stairs, her head bent over the armload of roses.

Chapter 22

"Are you going to marry Frank?"

Mom looked up from the bran muffin she was buttering. "Of course not," she laughed. "What a silly question! Frank and I are just friends."

Garren stabbed at his floating cereal, shoving the colorful circles deep into the milk.

Mom got up and set her empty plate in the sink. "Look, Frank is just a nice guy. We talk when he comes into the bookstore. That's all there is to it."

"Does Dad know about him?" Garren could feel Mom's eyes on him, and sensed her rising anger.

"How should I know? I certainly don't keep track of his friends! God knows what he and Jake do on weekends."

What did she mean by that?

"Listen, baby." Her voice was softer. "Your dad and I are living separate lives now. That means different friends, too."

"Do you still love Dad?"

Her answer was slow in coming. "Yes. I guess I always will."

Garren could tell by Mom's tone of voice that the conversation was over. He looked at the roses, their velvety blossoms making the kitchen smell as though someone had just sprayed perfume. So what if Frank and not Dad had sent Mom flowers? She said she loved Dad, didn't she? But for the first time, Garren wondered if loving someone was enough.

"How many more meets before conference?" Dad asked. He reached for the catsup, covering his hominy and chicken fried steak. Overhead, country music blared from ceiling speakers. Garren liked coming to the truck stop, seeing the big eighteen-wheelers roll in with their loads of steel or produce or even pigs. Once they had seen a whole truckful of Christmas trees.

"One more. Conference is a week from Saturday. In Goldsborough Gym." Garren took a drink of his chocolate shake. *You'll come, won't you?* he wanted to say. But instead he waited.

"A week from Saturday, hmmm . . ." Dad took out the small calendar he carried in his pocket. Garren listened to the sounds of silverware clattering, the *whoosh* of air brakes outside. He listened to his own heart beating. He listened— and tried not to hope. "Oh, can you believe it!" Dad slammed the calendar down on the table. "I have a sales seminar that day. In Chicago. Won't get back until late."

Garren looked into Dad's face and tried to read the look he saw there. Was it regret? Guilt? Or was he glad he didn't have to come and sit all day on hard bleachers in a smelly gym?

"I'm really sorry, sport." Dad put the calendar away and began spreading jam on his biscuit. "Any real competition?"

"Lynchburg," Garren said, pushing his plate away. "He's won almost all his matches this year."

"Yes, but *you're* undefeated! You already beat him once—"

"But it was close. Real close."

"You can do it! I have confidence in you." Dad picked up the check and reached for his wallet.

Then come and watch me. Garren opened his mouth, but the words wouldn't come. "Is it an important sales seminar?" he

116

asked finally as they walked past displays of CB's and cowboy boots.

"Really big. Because I'm district manager I have to do a presentation. And I can't very well demand that my salesmen be there if I cut out, now can I?" He laughed and shook his head.

Garren stared down at his fraying shoestring. The whole end had unraveled into scrawny strings that dragged across the linoleum. *Work comes first. It always has.* The thing that amazed Garren was that this fact still hurt.

Dad seemed to sense Garren's mood. He stopped beside the long row of pay phones and put his hand on Garren's shoulder. "You're really upset about this, aren't you, sport?"

"It's conference, Dad! The biggest wrestling meet of the year."

"I know. And I'm sorry. I don't schedule these infernal seminars, but I do have to attend them. It's part of my job." Garren didn't look up. "There'll be other wrestling meets— and I'll be there for them. You'll see." Dad ruffled Garren's hair. "Hang tough and show this Lynchburg character what you're made of! And I'll call you the minute I get in from Chicago."

Phone calls and promises. Garren felt like his whole life was made up of these two things.

Garren's arm shook as he did one-handed push-ups. "Four, five, six." He collapsed onto his rug, heart pounding in his ears.

"Quite a workout, kid." Herbie tossed a towel down to Garren. "Trying to break the world's record for the number of muscles strained in one day?"

Garren sat up and wiped the sweat off his arms. "No, just trying to make sure I can beat Lynchburg with one hand tied behind my back."

"If I were you, I'd plan on using both hands," Herbie said. "And both arms and both legs and—"

"How about a little 'heavenly help'?" Garren teased.

"You want I should break his leg?" Herbie asked in his tough-guy voice.

"No, nothing so drastic. How about giving him a case of the measles? Or maybe he could just oversleep—by a couple of days."

"Right. I can see me explaining that one to the Boss!" Herbie waved the idea aside with his hand. "Besides, you're ready. I've watched every match, and you've been wrestling great all season."

"Yeah, and Dad's only seen two of them." Garren rolled up his rug and stashed it under the bed. "I'd give anything if he'd come, Herbie. I'm doing this for him—him and Mom. I know once I get 'Most Valuable Wrestler' everything will be different. I've seen it in my head a thousand times. They'll be so proud, standing there together. . . ."

"Look, kid, sometimes things don't work out just like you want—"

"No!" Garren yelled. "It's going to work! I know it! Mom and Dad are a couple. They always have been. And nobody can change that—not Frank and his dumb flowers or Jake with his stupid spare room." Garren felt the lump in his throat, the stinging in his eyes. He ran down the hall and into the bathroom.

Not until he was in the shower did he let the tears come.

Chapter 23

The rain fell in gray-blue sheets, pounding against the windshield of the car. Mom switched the wipers to high. "Such a morning! What was that little rhyme we used to say about 'March winds and April showers'?"

"I dunno, Mom." Garren stretched and yawned. Weigh-ins were always so early! And he was starving. All day yesterday he'd tried not to eat, afraid he wouldn't make weight. But as soon as he was registered and weighed, he was going to head for concessions. "Suppose the hot dogs are ready yet?"

"Oh, Garren! How can you even think about hot dogs this time of morning?" Mom wrinkled up her nose in disgust.

"With mustard and catsup and relish. And onions. Lots of onions." Garren grinned as Mom shook her head.

They pulled up outside Goldsborough Gym. Garren reached for his bag. "Be careful, baby," Mom said. Garren had been wrestling for five years, but Mom still couldn't get used to the idea. In the beginning, she'd tried coming to the meets but was miserable the whole time. Every grunt and groan seemed to cause her pain. And the occasional nosebleeds were more than she could stand.

"Don't worry," Garren said. "I'm gonna float like a

butterfly and sting like a bee!" Then, laughing, he threw the car door open and plunged into the rain.

The gym was already filling up. As Garren bounded up the steps to the weigh-in room, he was almost sure he could smell hot dogs cooking.

The bleachers seemed to swarm with people. The gym was hot, and Garren was beginning to wish he'd eaten only one hot dog. He sat in a corner, watching his teammates wrestle and waiting for his weight to be called. Lynchburg walked by, but he didn't notice Garren. Garren watched the muscles in Lynchburg's legs as he moved down the sidelines. Lynchburg was tough, no doubt about it.

"No tougher than you are, kid." Herbie hovered overhead, fanning himself with his halo. "So this is what a conference wrestling tourney looks like."

"Impressed?"

Herbie shrugged. "You forget how long I've been around. I remember the Olympics when they were a newfangled idea. Still, there is a kind of grand feel to this competition."

Just then they called Garren's weight. He took his time getting to staging. He'd seen the bout sheets and knew he had to wrestle three times before he got a chance at Lynchburg. And the championship. But he'd seen enough reversals and quick pins to know that every match was important, every opponent potentially lethal.

"Gillum!" the pairing master yelled.

"Here!" Garren stepped off the bleachers and reached for the bout sheet. Finally, it was here. Conference tourney. The moment he'd been working and waiting for. He could feel the energy pounding through his biceps, surging against his calves. *Win, pin. Win, pin.* Winning had never been so important.

"Let's hear it for Gillum—the next wrestling champion of the world!"

Garren looked up from the bout sheet he was signing.

Ears waved from the top bleacher. His hand shaking, Garren wrote his name on the "winner" line. One down. Literally. A solid pin, and in less than a minute. He took the sheet to the tournament master and then went upstairs to see Ears.

"Good job, man!" Ears said, his grin almost reaching from one earphone to the other. "Maybe you should turn pro and let me manage you! We'll give you a catchy name—something like Gut Gillum. And when the offers to do TV commercials come in . . ."

Garren laughed. "First I've got to win conference."

"No problem!" Ears said.

"What about Lynchburg?"

"Piece of cake!"

"Marble cake," Garren said. "He's hard as a rock. Probably benches two hundred."

"Don't think about that kind of stuff. Just think how good it's going to feel to push his back into the mat."

Garren smiled. That *would* feel pretty good. If he could just make it happen.

The day passed slowly. Garren's team was in third place. Mosier was on a winning streak, would probably take his division. Ears stayed for the first two matches, but then had to leave for a dentist appointment. Garren went outside with him to see him off.

"Break a leg!" Ears said, retrieving his skateboard from behind a shrub. The rain had stopped now and everything looked a fresh, lime-colored green.

"That's how you wish actors good luck, not wrestlers!" Garren groaned.

"Whatever!" Ears said, popping in a fresh tape. "Kick his butt good!" Then, with a wave, he plunked down his skateboard and coasted across the parking lot, dodging buses and cars and assorted pieces of litter.

Garren was waiting on deck for his next match when he heard it. Clearly. Someone close by in the bleachers was calling his name. But who? Ears was gone.

"Get 'em, Garren! Show your stuff!"

The voice was deep and familiar. It sounded like . . . no, it couldn't be Dad. If this was Herbie's idea of a joke . . .

Garren turned and scanned the bleachers, searching. Just when he was about to give up, a faded "Cubs" sweatshirt caught his eye. Dad! Garren blinked in disbelief.

Dad waved. "Go for it, Son!"

Garren felt a rush of excitement. Dad was here! He stepped onto the mat, eyeing his opponent. Wiry. But scared. Garren could see it in his eyes.

Nothing Dad likes better than a solid takedown and a quick pin, Garren thought as the referee blew his whistle. And Garren didn't disappoint him.

Garren and Dad sat in the canteen, sharing an order of nachos. "I can't believe you're here," Garren said, licking cheese off his fingers. "What happened about the meeting in Chicago?"

Dad smiled. "I guess they're still having it. They're just having it without me."

Garren looked at Dad, waiting for the explanation.

"It's all pretty strange, actually," Dad said, pushing the remaining chips toward Garren. "I got up early this morning so I'd have plenty of time. Well, it was raining cats and dogs! And when I got down to my car, I had a flat tire. Brand new tires they are, too! Jake doesn't have a garage, so I had to change it in the rain. By the time I was finished, I looked like some half-drowned stray pup."

From far away came the sound of Herbie's laughter. *I wonder if Herbie . . .*

"I came upstairs and flicked on the radio while I changed clothes. Well, the announcer kept talking about how backed-up the tollway was. About the accidents on the Dan Ryan. And how a semi had just jack-knifed across the very exit I was headed for." Dad shook his head. "The whole idea of getting to that seminar seemed hopeless. And kind of silly. I knew by the time I got there it would be too late for my presentation. And if my salesmen were going, they were there already. My tearing in two hours late wouldn't make any difference." He paused for a moment, studying the ice cubes in his cup. When he looked up at Garren, there was a tenderness in his face. "Besides, here was where I really wanted to be. In Goldsborough Gym. Watching my son take first place." Dad sighed. "That flat tire and traffic jam reminded me that some things are even more important than sales seminars."

It was a long speech for Dad. Garren knew he should say something back, but what? He knew he could never in a million years find the words to tell Dad how glad he was that he'd come. How good it felt to know that, just for today, work didn't come first. But something in Dad's smile when he punched Garren on the shoulder told Garren he didn't have to say a word.

Garren felt a thousand pins stabbing into his spine. But still he pushed, arched, bridged until Lynchburg at last rolled off him. *Too tough to hurt.* Coach's words echoed in Garren's mind. *Be too tough to hurt.* In a flash Garren was on his feet, crouched. Waiting for Lynchburg to make his move. He didn't have long to wait. Lynchburg shot, but the dive was shallow and Garren ended up on top. Sweat melted into sweat as the two rolled, each trying for the advantage. The score . . . what was the score? When Garren last looked, he had been behind. It didn't matter. What mattered was the next second and the next one after that. Defend. Attack. Garren worked his way out of a headlock, caught Lynchburg in a cradle. He could hear his Dad's voice above the din of the crowd. "Come on, Son. You can do it!"

Garren knew there couldn't be much time left. Now. Move. He willed his legs and arms into a unified assault. Throw a soup from behind. Follow up with a half. Lynchburg was on his back, gasping. Garren tugged the head up, forced the shoulder blades into the mat. Deeper. Deeper. Every muscle screamed. Time stood still. And then, when

Garren knew he couldn't hold on a second longer, the ref's hand slapped the mat—just as the towel sailed across the mat. A pin! Garren rolled off Lynchburg and lay on the mat, the wired ceiling lights glaring down on him. He'd done it. He'd won conference!

Garren and Lynchburg stumbled to the center of the mat where the referee held Garren's hand high. "The winner!" he yelled.

Clapping. From everywhere it seemed. Even Lynchburg said, "Nice match." Coach was smiling and Mosier was whooping. But it was Dad Garren searched out. And it was Dad's arms that caught him at the edge of the mat, that held him when his knees gave way. He leaned his head into Dad's chest.

Garren couldn't remember ever being so happy.

Chapter

24

"It's beautiful!" Elise held the medal by its red-white-and-blue ribbon. It turned slowly, the two gold wrestlers etched into its middle flashing in the light.

"It is, isn't it?" Garren laughed, taking the medal from her outstretched hand and carefully folding it into his jean jacket pocket. He noticed a stack of record albums and tape boxes on the floor behind Elise's chair. "What's this stuff?" He picked up the stack and began looking through them. Mostly old songs from the fifties. A few classical pieces with grand pianos on the cover. And more Beatles albums than he knew existed. "Whose are these?"

Elise looked away, her answer almost a whisper. "Mine."

"Great! Let's play a few—" Garren was instantly sorry. Dumb. He was glad Elise had been turned away and couldn't read his lips. These were Elise's before . . . before she became deaf. But why did she have them out now? He wanted to ask, but something told him to wait.

Reaching for the stack of albums, Elise said, "I've always loved music. My favorite toy when I was little was one of those flutes with half a dozen holes." She laughed. "I used to give concerts for my folks, and I always insisted on a standing ovation at the end." She ran her finger around the corner of a Beethoven sonata album. "I started piano when I was four and played in my first recital a year later."

"Do you still play?"

"Sometimes. I can sort of feel the music, especially the rumble of the bass notes. But it's hard to remember the melodies."

"Will you play something for me sometime?"

"Maybe."

They sat in silence, the only sound the dripping of rain from a leak in the gutter. It made Garren sad to think that Elise couldn't even hear that.

"You miss listening to your collection, don't you?"

Elise nodded. "But I miss lots of things now that I'm . . . deaf." She swallowed hard, as though the word had left a bad taste in her mouth. "I miss the sounds of the wind and the sea. I always loved the *whoosh* and *splash* when we went to the beach. I miss the sounds of telephones and doorbells and toasters popping up. But most of all I miss the sound of people's voices. I miss that so much sometimes I ache." She wrapped her arms around herself and looked into Garren's face. "I don't even know what your voice sounds like."

Garren sat up straight and lowered his voice. "Actually, it's a lot like John Wayne and Clint Eastwood, with a little of Sylvester Stallone and Patrick Swayze thrown in for good measure."

Elise laughed. "That's just the way I imagined it."

A crack of thunder rattled the windowpane. Elise jumped. "Did you hear that?"

"More like felt it. Vibrations."

Garren had an idea. He picked up a Beatles album. "You do dance, don't you?"

Elise narrowed her eyes. "What?"

Garren said each word carefully. "You do dance, don't you?"

"Dance?"

Garren went to the stereo and raised the dustcover. Carefully he adjusted the bass to the maximum level. Then he turned up the volume and carefully set the needle down on the record.

"I wanna hold your ha-ha-hand, I wanna hold your hand." The speakers pumped out noise. Lamp shades seemed to vibrate; the walls almost wobbled.

Elise sat on the edge of her chair, looking like she didn't know whether to blush or giggle. Garren moved toward her, keeping time to the music with his feet. Slowly, a smile spread across her face. She watched Garren dance around her, and he motioned for her to get up. Shaking her head, she sank deeper into her seat, but he grabbed her hand and pulled her to her feet. She stood rooted to the hardwood floor. "*Feel* it!" He wiggled his hips. "Dance!"

"You look silly!" she said. But slowly, she began to shuffle her feet. The booming bass rhythm accelerated. So did Elise's movements. Little by little, she loosened up. Soon she was dancing and laughing along with Garren, making up silly moves and trying to bump him into the furniture. When the scratch of the needle signaled the end of that side, Garren went to the stereo and clicked it off. Elise fell onto the couch, giggling.

"Thanks," she said when she could finally speak.

"My pleasure." Garren bowed from the waist, tipping an imaginary hat.

"How about a root beer float?" Elise asked, heading for the kitchen.

"How are things with your parents?"

Garren scooped a spoonful of foam from the top of his float. "About the same, I guess. We keep going to the counselor, and I think talking with her makes us all feel better. But Mom and Dad don't talk to each other much. They always have me give messages to the other one. 'Tell your father that that dentist's bill has to be paid.' Or 'Tell your mother that I'll be picking you up early on Sunday.' Sometimes I feel like the U.S. Post Office!"

Elise didn't say anything for a few moments. Then she

asked hesitantly, "Do you think . . . your Dad . . . might be coming back home?"

Garren didn't answer right away. He thought about the coldness between Mom and Dad. About Frank's flowers. About the argument he'd overheard at Christmas. But Mom had said she loved Dad. And there was still the awards banquet—still the chance that once they were together for a while . . . "Maybe," he said, shrugging. He was glad when Elise didn't ask any more questions.

They were almost finished with their drinks when Elise asked, "Know how a blind man knows when he's done?"

Garren shook his head.

Elise sucked hard on her straw, making loud, slurping sounds till all she sucked was air. "That's how! Know how a deaf man knows when he's done?"

Again Garren shook his head.

This time Elise lifted the glass and put it up to her eye. Her features looked exaggerated and comical through its thick bottom, and Garren laughed. But it was a laugh that faded quickly. "How can you make jokes about being deaf?" Garren asked as they put their glasses in the sink.

"Sometimes laughing about it takes some of the pain away." She ran water in the two glasses. Then she turned around and said slowly, "I'm going away as soon as school is out."

Garren looked at her in surprise. "Why? Where? For how long?"

Elise sat back down at the table. "To Boston. To see a doctor. Maybe have an operation."

"What kind of operation?" Garren imagined surgeons and knives and a hospital room where they would hook Elise up to millions of tubes and monitors. "When did you find out about this?"

"I guess I've known it was coming for a long time," Elise sighed. "The audiologist who tested me that first day at the school for the hearing impaired seemed surprised when I told him I'd never been to a specialist. Just ol' Doc Smyth, who always gave me this horrible-tasting medicine for my colds and yellow drops for my earaches. Well, he had Father come in for a conference. He told him he thought my hearing could be helped . . . maybe a lot . . . with surgery. Father wouldn't hear of it at first. He thought it would just get my hopes up and do more harm than good. But finally, last month, he took me to a specialist."

"And?" Garren asked, his heart beating faster.

"And he said I had otosclerosis, something wrong with the bones in my ears."

"Can they fix it?"

Elise shrugged. "He seems to think so. But Father wants a second opinion. He once taught at a university with the man who now heads up the Boston Clinic—so that's where we're going." Elise pushed her chair back from the table and stood up. "Anyway, we leave the day after school is out."

"How long will you be gone?" Garren was glad Elise couldn't hear how shaky his voice was.

"Couple of weeks, if everything goes okay."

"Oh, it will. It will go just fine!" Garren wasn't sure if he was trying to convince Elise or himself.

Elise smiled and patted his arm. "Don't look so worried. The worst that can happen is I get to see Boston. And the best thing that can happen is . . ." Elise could hardly speak the best thing. "I may be able to hear again."

Garren managed to grin. "That's what I'm worried about."

Elise could see the mischief in his face. "Really?"

"Yeah," he said, slipping on his jean jacket and pausing at the door. "Then you'll find out I sound more like Kermit the Frog than Clint Eastwood!"

They laughed as he left. But their laughter was tight, forced—and couldn't cover up the fact that they were both scared about the future.

Chapter

Garren stood at the mirror, adjusting his tie. Usually he hated wearing ties, but tonight he didn't mind. Not even the thought of wearing those tight black dress shoes could dampen his enthusiasm. Tonight was the awards banquet. And Garren was to be honored as "Most Valuable Wrestler!"

"Sharp. Very sharp," Herbie said as Garren slid his belt through the loops. His conference medal lay on the dresser. "Going to wear this, too?"

"Coach asked me to bring it." Garren slid the medal into his front pocket. "I can't believe it's finally here, Herbie."

"That's the way life is, kid. The things you think will last forever—like that unit on fractions you had in math last year—end. And things you think will never get here, are over before you know it."

"Well, this night is the beginning, not the end."

Herbie got a worried look on his face. "Listen, kid . . ."

But Garren didn't have time to listen, for just then Dad honked the horn outside.

He met Mom in the hallway. She looked great. Her soft blue dress matched the color of her eyes. *Wait till Dad sees her*, Garren thought as they went down the stairs together.

"I can't believe that garage didn't have my car ready!"

Mom fussed as she locked the front door behind them. "The mechanic promised me!"

"It's okay, Mom," Garren said. "I'm sure Dad didn't mind picking us up." Garren followed her down the walk toward the car. Everything was working out just the way Garren had hoped. Mom and Dad together . . .

Mom opened the door and climbed into the back seat. *The back seat!* Garren was so stunned, it took him a minute to react. "Sit up here, Mom! I'll sit in back."

"No, no," Mom said, shaking her head. "You and your Dad can talk better this way. I'm fine."

Garren looked at Dad. He didn't seem to mind that Mom was sitting in back. He patted the seat beside him. "Hey, champ! Let's get going. They can't start this party without the guest of honor!" He laughed.

Garren slid in beside his dad and slammed the car door shut. This wasn't the way he'd planned things. But there was plenty of time yet. He and Mom and Dad had all evening . . .

The cafeteria swarmed with parents and kids. It seemed strange to see everybody so dressed up when usually they wore old sweats or team singlets.

Garren and his parents stood in the entry to the room, looking around. Then Garren spotted Coach heading toward them with his hand extended. He nudged his dad.

"Mr. Gillum," Coach said, "we're so glad you could come!" He shook Dad's hand for a long time. "Got yourself a real winner here." He nodded toward Garren.

"Yes, I'm very proud of him," Dad said.

"We're *both* proud of him," Mom said, her voice taking on the icy edge Garren hadn't heard in a while.

"Of course, of course!" Coach laughed, moving on to greet the next set of parents.

Dad looked at Mom but didn't say anything.

"We better find our seats," Garren said, stepping between them and steering them toward the table reserved for those receiving special awards. "You sit here," he said to Mom, pulling out a chair in the middle of the long row. She smiled and sat down. "And, Dad, you sit here." Garren patted the back of the chair next to Mom. For a moment Dad hesitated, then he pulled out the chair and sat down. Garren walked around the table and sat across from them—across from the *two* of them. Mom and Dad sitting side by side—it looked just as good as he'd imagined.

"Hey, Gillum!" It was Mosier, waving from the other end of the table. Garren waved back. Slowly, the tables filled up. Mom talked to Garren; Dad talked to Garren. But even though they were sitting side by side, they didn't talk to each other. Garren began turning his fork over and over on the tablecloth. This wasn't exactly the way he'd planned things. He had to do something. But what? "Dad," he said, laying down his fork, "tell Mom that story you told me last week, about how you almost got to meet Larry Byrd."

Dad started to smile, but then the creases in his forehead deepened, and he ended up with a crooked frown on his face. "Your mom's not interested, Garren."

Mom glared at Dad. "Really? And how do you know?"

"I just know. You were never interested in sports."

"Then why did I spend four years as a cheerleader?"

"How should I know!" Dad huffed.

"I thought you knew everything—"

Garren cleared his throat. "Hope they don't serve the same stuff we have to eat when *we* come in here." He tried to laugh, but it came out more like a cough.

"I'm sure it will be just fine," Mom said, reaching across the table to pat his hand.

The meal was spaghetti, and Garren spent most of the time trying not to get sauce on his tie. He gave his salad to Mom and his garlic bread to Dad. He felt like his stomach was already full—full of butterflies.

Soon the program started. Coach took the microphone. "On behalf of the Hinkle Creek athletic department, I want to thank you all for coming tonight." Coach laid his stack of note cards on the podium and fumbled for something inside his suit jacket pocket. With an embarrassed smile, he slipped on his glasses. A ripple of laughter ran through the crowd. It wasn't often the boys saw Coach Cannon looking so intellectual! "We've had a fine season, and each one of you has reason to be proud. Wrestling is more than a sport; it's a mind-set."

Garren had heard this same speech last year. But it was a pretty good speech, and Garren half-listened, the way he sometimes half-watched reruns on TV. But mostly he looked at Mom and Dad. At the way her hair curled onto her cheek. At the way his tie wrinkled up just above his tie tack. He looked at them together, framed the picture in his mind. Willed himself to remember every detail. The green paper napkin Mom held wadded in her hand. The way the light shimmered off Dad's big gold watch. *This is the beginning of lots of evenings the three of us will spend together.* Garren wished he could say those words out loud, could taste their sweetness on his tongue and hear them with his own ears. *This is the beginning of lots of evenings together.* He closed his eyes and tried to believe it was true.

Awards. Clapping. Awards. Clapping. The evening moved from "Most Promising First-Year Wrestler" to "Most Improved" to "Most Aggressive." Mosier got an award for "Most Take-Downs." Finally, there was only one award left. *What am I so nervous about?* Then he looked across at Mom and Dad—and he knew.

"Finally, the highest award given in Hinkle Creek Wrestling. This award is given only to the most worthy of contestants—to the boy who is a model of sportsmanship, who exhibits team spirit, who gives two-hundred percent." Mom looked across at Garren and smiled. " 'Most Valuable Wrestler' is an honor not easily earned, not lightly esteemed."

Garren tried to remember if he'd heard this speech before, too. But it didn't matter. It sounded fine—just fine.

"Tonight this award goes to an undefeated wrestler, to

133

one who has taken on all competitors, and soundly defeated each one."

Garren thought about Lynchburg. *Wonder if he'll be "Most Valuable" at his school?*

"It is with great pride that I present this year's 'Most Valuable Wrestler Award' to Garren Gillum!"

The clapping began loud and got louder. Garren pushed back his chair and walked toward the podium to claim his prize.

"Get 'em, Gillum!" Whistles and foot stomping. Thunderous applause. Garren felt the butterflies disappear, and a warm happiness take their place.

When Garren reached the podium, Coach grabbed his

hand and pumped it up and down. "Congratulations," he said, handing him a huge plaque with his name engraved in gold lettering.

Garren smiled, grateful he didn't have to say anything. Then, just as he turned to go back to his seat, people all over the room began standing up. First his teammates, then the parents. A standing ovation. Garren was being given a standing ovation! He paused, unsure what to do. He looked at Mosier, who was clapping louder than anybody. Then he looked toward his parents.

It was the scene he had imagined a thousand times. Mom's eyes were moist, her face glowing with pride. Dad stood tall beside her, his big hands applauding, that wonderful grin taking up his whole face. Garren wanted to freeze everything, the way the "pause" button on the VCR could hold a scene forever. He began walking, the plaque clutched close to his chest, pride and embarrassment swelling inside him. Then, just before he reached his seat, he saw it. Mom and Dad's shoulders touched. For just an instant. Mom pulled away; Dad didn't seem to notice.

One by one, the crowd sat down. Garren was glad to see that Dad was the last one to take his seat.

"I'm hungry," Garren said as they walked across the parking lot to Dad's car.

"We just came from an awards *banquet!*" Mom laughed.

"I know. But I was too nervous to eat." Garren made sure he got in the back seat this time.

Dad held the door for Mom, then walked around to the driver's side and got in. "We could stop off at Family Tree. I could use some coffee. How about it?" He looked at Garren's mother. She checked her watch.

Please, Mom, Garren thought. *Please say yes!*

"Well, if we don't stay too long. Garren does have school tomorrow."

Family Tree. Garren smiled into the darkness of the back seat. Sounded like a good place for a family to eat.

"I'll take the double cheeseburger, an order of onion rings, and a chocolate shake." Garren folded the menu and handed it to the waitress. Dad ordered pie and coffee. Mom ordered a diet cola.

"That's quite a plaque you got tonight," Dad said, stirring sugar into his coffee. "Where will you hang it?"

Garren took a long drink of his milk shake. "Someplace in my room. Maybe over the bed."

"You sure had a great season, sport!" Dad shook his head and whistled. "Undefeated!"

"I'm just glad he didn't get hurt," Mom said.

Dad stopped stirring and looked up at her. "Aren't you just a little glad he won?"

Mom's back stiffened. "Of course I'm glad he won! Why would I let him put in all those long hours and do those painful workouts if I didn't want him to win?"

All around them people were eating, talking in soft voices, laughing. *Why can't we be like that?* Garren wondered, stacking up the little packets of cream the waitress had left on the table.

Dad turned to Garren. "What now, sport? Going to try for Junior Olympic Wrestling?"

Garren shrugged just as the tower of cream toppled. "Some pretty tough competition there, I bet."

"And lots of chances to get hurt, too." Mom poked her straw into the crushed ice filling up her glass.

"All you ever think about is that he'll get hurt!" Dad's voice was louder than it needed to be. He kept stirring his coffee.

"All you care about is winning—at any price. And I'm not just talking about sports, either."

Dad threw his spoon down on the table. "Now what's that supposed to mean?"

People were beginning to stare.

"It means you think competition is everything."

"You think it's not? It's a dog-eat-dog world out there! A man's got to fight for every break he gets. And the sooner Garren realizes that, the better!"

136

"What about kindness and generosity? What about taking time to be with people you care about? Don't those things count for anything? What you know about life could be shoved into one of your stupid shoe samples!"

"You don't know what the world's like. Besides, kindness won't put bread on the table."

A sarcastic smile crossed Mom's face. "So, we're back to money. Always back to money."

"Well, love sure doesn't make the world go 'round."

"One double cheeseburger and onion rings." The waitress plopped the plate down in front of Garren. But he knew, even as she left to bring him the catsup, that he couldn't eat. The butterflies in his stomach had turned into pains. All he wanted to do was go home.

"I . . . I don't feel so good."

Instantly Mom's hand was on Garren's forehead. "No fever."

Dad gave a disgusted grunt. "Don't give up hope. Maybe one will develop."

Mom slid out of the booth and Garren followed her.

"Sorry, Dad."

Dad brushed the apology aside with a wave of his hand. "Don't worry about it, Son. It's been a full evening."

The waitress brought the check and Mom picked it up. "I'll take care of this."

"Now just a minute!" Dad said, grabbing it out of her hand. "I'm paying!" Dad was yelling now, and Garren could feel the stares of the other customers.

"Too bad you're not as eager to pay some of the other bills you owe." Mom turned her back and, taking Garren's arm, pushed him toward the door.

Tossing a ten-dollar bill down on the table, Dad hurried after them, his fists clenched.

Garren sat in the front seat again. He closed his eyes against the lights of approaching traffic. Against the coldness that filled the car.

It was a very long ride home.

Chapter 26

"And then what happened?"

Garren stood looking into Mrs. Adney's aquarium, watching the zebra fish swimming in circles. "And then we went home—Mom and me." He turned around to face her, glad that these months of counseling sessions had made it easier to talk. "It was a weird evening."

Mrs. Adney leaned across the desk toward him. "Weird in what way?"

Garren thought about it. "It was like the best and worst night of my life."

"What do you mean?"

"Well, it was kind of like being on a roller coaster ride. One minute I felt on top of the world—seeing Mom and Dad together, winning 'Most Valuable Wrestler.' Then the next minute I felt all scared, like things were out of control. Like we were in a movie, but everyone kept saying the wrong lines."

"Garren," Mrs. Adney said, "why do you suppose your parents fight?"

"Because they're mad at each other. All the time." He kicked at his frayed shoelace. "And because of me."

"Because of you?"

"Mom tries to baby me too much. And Dad . . . well, Dad is always in high gear. Rushing off somewhere. Pushing himself—and other people, too." Garren sighed. "I keep trying to figure out what to do to make them both happy. I thought winning that award would fix things up. I was sure that once they were both together . . . Maybe if I made the principal's honor roll every grading period, things would be different."

Mrs. Adney came from behind her desk and put her arm around Garren. They walked across her office and sat in the big leather chairs, facing the window. "Garren, I'm going to tell you something you may have trouble believing, but it's true." She waited for Garren to look at her. Then she said, slowly and deliberately, "There is nothing you can do to change things between your mother and father."

Garren looked away, clenching his fists against the soft arm of the chair. *Oh yes there is!* he thought. *I just have to figure out what!*

Mrs. Adney was still talking. ". . . kids I talk to feel this way. The separation wasn't your fault, Garren. You didn't cause it—and you can't fix it, either."

Garren tried not to hear, tried not to believe what she said was true. He tried to think up a new plan. Something so sensational that Mom and Dad would have to be impressed, would want them to all be a family again. But no ideas came. Only the memory of Mom and Dad fighting. In the car. In the cafeteria. In the restaurant. "Why do they have to fight all the time?" Garren realized he had asked it out loud.

"Your parents aren't really fighting about you. And they're not fighting about money or visitation rights or your dad's job."

"They're not? It sure sounds that way!"

"What really makes them angry, the thing they're really fighting about, is their inability to get along. Because they find it impossible to be polite and kind to each other, the way they once were, they react with hostility."

Garren remembered what Coach Cannon always said. "You mean the best defense is a good offense?"

Mrs. Adney chuckled. "In sports, maybe. But in relationships, it doesn't work quite so well."

Garren picked up the wrestling medal and plaque he'd brought to show her. "These aren't worth anything if Mom and Dad can't get back together."

Mrs. Adney reached for the medal, cradling it in her palm. "I know one of the reasons you wanted to win 'Most Valuable Wrestler' was so the three of you could go to the awards banquet together. But there were other reasons, too."

"What reasons?"

"You're a good team member, Garren," she said, slipping the medal around his neck. "You worked hard to win for the team. And you worked hard for yourself, too—to prove to yourself that you could be undefeated, that you could beat . . . what was his name?"

"Lynchburg."

"Yes, Lynchburg. You were trying to make both your parents proud of you—and you did! That plaque represents work and dedication, determination and team spirit. It's a wonderful award, one you'll cherish for the rest of your life."

The rest of my life. Garren hadn't thought much beyond the end of wrestling season, much beyond that magical moment when Mom and Dad would be together at the awards banquet. But the banquet hadn't been so magical after all.

And now there was, as Mrs. Adney had pointed out, the rest of his life.

Chapter

27

"Summer league sign-ups are two weeks from Saturday." Ears threw a grounder and Garren bent over to scoop it up.

"Already?"

"I'm tired of playing shortstop. Think I'd make a good outfielder?"

"Sure. You could grab the ball and then ride your skateboard into infield before you threw it."

Ears grinned. "If we sign up together, maybe we can be on the same team again."

Garren tossed the ball high, and Ears dropped back for the catch. It landed in his glove with a solid *plop*. "I don't know if I'm going to play this summer."

Ears stopped his windup. "You must be kidding. We always play summer league!"

Garren pulled off his glove and headed for the porch. "Well, just because we've always done it doesn't mean I have to keep on doing it."

"But you like it! And you're a great second baseman!" Ears followed close at his heels.

"Maybe I've got more important things to worry about than whether a runner is out or not."

"Let me guess," Ears said, sitting down on the top step. "You're going to Washington to advise the Pentagon about the arms race. Or maybe address Congress on the national debt. No, no . . . I know! You've agreed to be the first teenage astronaut and NASA is putting you in training this summer."

Garren pulled at his shoestring, fraying it even more. "Very funny. It's just that things will be . . . well, different this summer."

"You mean your folks? Come on, Garren. Your dad never made that many of the games anyway."

How can I make him understand? Garren wondered. How could he tell him that even though Dad didn't come to every game, he at least came home at night. And then, when Mom was busy in the kitchen, Garren would tell him about the whole game, play-by-play like a sports announcer. How could he tell Ears—whose family was so normal their favorite ice cream was vanilla—that he was scared what life might be like if Mom and Dad didn't get back together. Afraid that people in the bleachers would be clicking their tongues in sympathy and saying, "See that second baseman? Poor boy. From a broken home. Parents just split up."

"Maybe I'll play and maybe I won't!"

"Okay, man!" Ears stood up and started down the steps for home. "You've still got two weeks to decide. Think about it!"

Think. That's all Garren did anymore. About Mom and Dad—and Jake and Frank. About how you take a family vacation when you're not a family anymore. About where he'd be living when school started next fall.

Garren was still sitting on the steps when the phone rang. He bounded through the kitchen and caught it on the third ring. "Hello," he said breathlessly.

"Mrs. Gillum, please." The voice was formal and very businesslike.

"She's not here. Could I take a message?"

The sound of papers rustling. "Is this Garren?" He said it

carefully, stretching out the vowel so the first syllable rhymed with "car."

Garren was surprised to hear his name from the stranger. "Yes."

"This is Mr. Babcock, your mother's lawyer."

Why did Mom's lawyer need to talk to her? All the separation details had been worked out months ago.

"Do you know when she'll be home?"

"I'm not sure. She's doing some errands after she gets off work." Again he offered, "Could I take a message?"

There was only a slight pause before the voice went on. "Yes, you may. Tell her they've set the court date."

Court date? "The court date for what?" Garren tried to keep his voice calm. Maybe Mom got a speeding ticket. Or was caught jaywalking in front of the mall.

"The divorce."

Garren went numb. Somehow he managed to finish the conversation and hang up. In a daze, he wandered to the family room and slumped onto the couch. Divorce. It was going to happen. It really was. After all those hours of counseling. After winning "Most Valuable Wrestler." After all his prayers. It was really going to happen.

Garren wanted to cry, but his eyes felt hollow. His whole body felt hollow, like the soap bubbles he used to blow when he was a kid. He'd always wondered if it hurt when they burst. Now he knew. *Too tough to hurt. Gotta be too tough to hurt*, he thought.

But Garren pulled his knees into his chest and cried anyway.

Mom nudged open the back door, one arm gripping a grocery bag, the other holding her freshly dry-cleaned suit. "What a lucky day I've had!" she greeted Garren, easing the bag onto the table and draping her suit over the back of a chair. "You know how you can never find a parking spot at the dry cleaners? Well, a man pulled out just as I turned the corner and I parked right in front of the door. And then I

143

went to the grocery to pick up a few things—well, they were having a two-for-one sale on almost half the items on my list!" She unsacked the food swiftly, her eyes bright. "But I've saved the best news for last. I'm getting a promotion! Assistant manager at the bookstore. Of course it will mean more hours, but it'll be more money, too. And a chance to advance to manager when the job opens up! I was so surprised. . . ."

Garren leaned against the refrigerator, waiting for her to stop talking. Waiting for her to notice that his world had fallen apart.

Finally she looked up, annoyed by Garren's silence. "Well, you could at least show some—" She looked into his pale face. "Baby, what's wrong?"

"I've got some news, too. You got a call."

Mom set down the cans of corn she was holding. "From whom?"

"Your lawyer."

Mom gripped the tops of the cans. And waited.

"He says they've set the court date. For the—" Garren tried to say the word, but he couldn't push it past the lump in his throat.

Mom's eyes were moist, but her face was calm. "It couldn't be helped. I'm sorry. We tried. God knows we tried! But it's over, baby. We've all got to accept that and get on with our lives."

She made it sound so simple, like tossing out an empty milk carton. *Get on with our lives.* Garren leaned his forehead against the cold metal trim on the refrigerator door.

Chapter

28

Two minutes till three. With any luck, Mr. Hoffer wouldn't give them an assignment. Garren already had homework in three classes—and it was Friday! The bell rang, and like a chain reaction of dominoes falling, two dozen books slammed shut. Garren was on his feet when Mr. Hoffer yelled, "Just a minute! I've got something for you."

Garren groaned. Not more homework!

Quickly, Mr. Hoffer handed a stack of yellow papers to the first person in each row. "Take this home with you. It's about your schedule for next year. You have some choices to make about classes. Think about it carefully. The counselor will begin seeing you on Monday, so make sure your decisions are made by then!" The class shuffled out, half-reading the papers as they merged into the crowded hall.

"I can't decide!" Garren lay stretched across his bed, the yellow sheet from the counselor in front of him. Herbie sat on his shoulder, looking over the choices with him. "Should I take shop or gym?"

"You did well in both this year. Would you rather build scale houses or muscles?" Herbie asked.

"And what am I going to do about art and music?"

"Which do you like better?"

"Art."

"Then check the box beside it."

"But music always takes field trips. Sometimes they miss the whole day!" Garren threw his pencil down on the bed. "I'm lousy at choices!"

"That's not true!" Herbie flew from his shoulder and perched on the headboard.

"Yes, it is." Garren rolled over on his side and propped his head on his hand. "Mom says she hates to take me to Ponderosa because I hold up the whole line at the buffet trying to decide what to put on my plate."

"Plates," Herbie corrected.

"If I can't decide what kind of dressing to put on my salad, how can I choose which courses I want next year? And the four years after that? I'm rotten at choices!"

Herbie flew down and sat cross-legged in mid-air near Garren, his wings still beating. "You've made lots of good choices this year!"

"Like what?"

"Well, there was deciding to ask Jennifer to the Christmas dance. And taking after-school help from Mr. Hoffer. There was the choice to make friends with Elise. And who could forget—the choice to cut your hair at the wrestling meet."

"That's one I'll never forget!" Garren was quiet for a moment. "What about the bad choices I've made?"

Herbie looked blank.

"Like forging Dad's name on my report card. And yelling at Mom every time I got upset about the separation."

"Forgotten. Completely and absolutely forgotten."

"Part of the 'angel oath'?"

"It's his policy," Herbie said, lifting his head heavenward as he spoke. "Forgive *and* forget. Always."

Garren chewed on the end of his pencil eraser as he reread the sheet. Herbie hovered above the schedule, reading it upside down.

"You know, kid, you've got some important decisions to make this year."

"You mean about enrichment or study hall?"

146

"No, about the divorce."

"I've got no choice in that! If I had, Mom and Dad would still be together."

"That's true. But you still have to choose."

"Choose what? I thought the courts had made all the decisions for me!"

"Only you can choose how you handle this whole thing—the divorce, the anger, the fear. You can let it gnaw at your gut till it eats you alive. Or you can face it head-on, like you did Lynchburg in that final match."

Garren held out his hand, and Herbie came to stand in his palm. "Herbie, why did God let my parents split up? Why didn't he get them back together? I prayed about it every night. You know I did!" Garren swallowed. "Is this his way of . . . of punishing me for something I did?"

Herbie shook his head. "No way, kid! Nobody loves you as much as he does. But God doesn't keep people on strings like marionettes, making them do everything he wants. You human beings are free creatures. Of course, God's there to help—but, in the end, people make their own decisions. Their own mistakes. Then they have to live with them. And so do the people they love." Herbie stepped on the bed and handed Garren his pencil. "So what's it going to be?"

Garren thought for a minute. "I always have lots of homework, so study hall would be nice. Coach says any sport helps every other sport, so taking gym will make me a better wrestler. And I guess I'd rather draw colorful pictures than play quarter notes." Garren checked the appropriate boxes. Then he filled out his name, address, phone number, and homeroom on the lines at the top of the paper. In the designated space, he wrote his parents' names. But he stopped cold at the next section, his pencil poised above the tiny squares. Married. Divorced.

Garren stared at the words for a long time, until the boxes in front of him blurred, until his eyes stung.

Then, blinking hard, he placed a firm X in the box beside "divorced."

Chapter 29

"I thought you weren't leaving until school was out!"

Elise sat down on the bottom step. "I wasn't supposed to, but Father's friend called to say there was an opening at the clinic." She bent to stroke the velvety petals of a peony growing beside the steps. "Besides," she sighed, "the sooner I go, the sooner it'll all be over with."

Garren didn't know what to say. He'd never had an operation—never even been in a hospital. What was Elise feeling? What would it be like to know that maybe—just maybe—your whole life was going to change? Or that you might have to go through all that pain for nothing? "I—I'll pray for you," Garren whispered.

Elise smiled, her eyes green as the new leaves that fluttered overhead. "Thanks."

Garren heard the bang of Elise's front door. He turned to see her father, surrounded by suitcases and with a road atlas squeezed under his arm. He called over to Garren, "We're ready to go. Please tell Elise."

Garren touched Elise's shoulder and pointed toward her house. Her father waved, motioning her home.

Elise stood up and brushed off the seat of her jeans. Carefully she signed, "Good-bye, my friend." Then she started down the walk.

Garren jumped to his feet. Impulsively, he picked the peony and raced after her. "Wait," he said, grabbing her elbow and turning her around. "Here." He opened her hand and laid the flower on her palm. "For luck," he signed.

Elise gave him a quick hug before she ran to help her father pack the car.

Garren was making himself a sandwich when the doorbell rang. He walked through the family room, taking big bites of bread and bologna and trying to figure out who was standing just out of sight on the porch. He pulled back the curtain and looked. Dad!

He flung open the door. Dad had on jeans and a sweatshirt. His hair stuck out from underneath a battered Cubs baseball hat. "Dad! What are you doing here?"

Dad stepped inside. "Came to see you. I called your mother at the bookstore, told her I was coming by. That we might take a ride out to the lake."

"Sure!" Garren stuffed the last of the sandwich in his mouth and ran to get his jacket.

Dad was quiet. He gripped the steering wheel like he was afraid it might try to escape at any minute. Garren watched the blur of trees and grass and pavement rush by outside his window. What was Dad thinking about? Was something wrong? Had he changed his mind about the divorce?

The beach was empty except for an old man playing Frisbee with his golden retriever. Dad parked close to the pavilion and got out. Garren followed him. Wind whipped the waves into white caps. Garren zipped his jacket against the chill. They walked for a while—Dad skipping stones, Garren kicking sand over an occasional dead fish. Finally they came to a big piece of driftwood and sat down. Garren ached to ask Dad what was wrong. But instead he waited, listening to the crash of waves, the screech of gulls. Finally, Dad spoke.

"Got something to tell you, sport." His face eased into a grin. "It's like those old jokes. I've got some good news and some bad news. Which do you want to hear first?"

Garren thought he'd had enough bad news to last him the rest of his life. "The good news."

"I've been promoted. Regional manager. Beat out over twenty contenders for the position. More responsibility. Bigger commissions. I even get a swanky office with windows and a secretary."

"Wow! That's great!" Garren tried to imagine what the bad news could be. It sounded perfect for Dad!

"Yeah." Dad skipped another stone. "I've worked fifteen years for this. No more hawking shoe samples to every two-bit store in the state. No more living on fast food and sleeping in cheap motels. This is the big time, Garren. My chance to really be somebody."

Garren wanted to congratulate Dad. To tell him how proud he was. But he sensed there was more to the story.

"Now, about that bad news," Dad sighed. "The region I'll be managing is . . . is on the East Coast."

East Coast? How could anybody live in Indiana and work on the East Coast? And then, in a wave of sickness that hit him in the stomach, Garren knew. Dad was moving. East. Forever.

Garren wanted to walk into the gray waves. To feel their coldness. To become nothing, like the sticks and pebbles that were washed up on shore. Dad. Moving. He put his head between his knees and dug a stick deep into the sand. Dad was still talking.

". . . leave real soon. Big training session starts next week. It's a great break for all of us. I'll have more money to send your mother. And I can help you pay for wrestling camp now. We'll see each other real often. I'll probably get to Chicago on business a lot. You can take the train in and meet me. And I'll fly you east on all your vacations. You'll probably get on a first-name basis with every stewardess between here and Boston." Dad tried to laugh.

Boston. That was where Elise was. *Small world*. Suddenly Garren remembered the globe his third-grade teacher kept on her desk. He'd loved to spin it around, watching countries and continents swirl past in splashes of colors. Everything looked so close, and for a long time he'd thought that was the way the world was. Now he knew better. Now he knew lots of things about the way the world was.

Boston. How far was that? Five hundred miles? A thousand? *Might as well be five million*. Five million . . . five million. The words repeated themselves, keeping time to the crashing of the waves, drowning out Dad's voice.

Chapter 30

Garren knelt in front of his opened locker, scooping mounds of paper into the hallway. What a mess! And final locker inspections were in ten minutes.

"Correct me if I'm wrong," Herbie said, pulling a crumpled paper from the pile, "but isn't this that math assignment you couldn't find last week?"

Garren grabbed the paper. "Sure is! I wonder if he'll take it late?" He smoothed out the wrinkles, folded it neatly, and stuck it in his back pocket. Herbie kicked a Zinger wrapper off the top shelf. It landed on Garren's head. "Hey, cut it out!" He brushed stray pieces of coconut out of his hair.

Herbie laughed, and the empty corridor echoed with its tinkling-clink. He kicked another piece of paper on Garren. Garren wadded up an old book report and threw it at Herbie. Soon papers were flying back and forth. Herbie created a mini tornado of gym shoes and gum wrappers and old tests. It swirled, Wizard-of-Oz style, around Garren.

"Enough! I give!" Garren yelled, covering his head and laughing. One by one the items dropped—trash into the metal can at the end of the hallway, shoes and books into Garren's open bag. The last echo of Herbie's laughter lingered in the hallway. "Hey, Herbie," Garren said, zipping his bag, "how come every time you laugh it sounds like wind chimes? Do all angels laugh like that?"

"Certainly not! Every angel gets to choose the sound of his laughter, his favorite sound in all creation. Wind chimes are mine."

"My favorite sound is a finely tuned motorcycle engine. Or maybe the sound of the ref's hand slapping the mat when I get a pin."

"Good thing you're not an angel!"

Garren and Herbie started down the hall. "Dad leaves in two days."

"I know."

"It's really a great opportunity for him." Garren bent over the drinking fountain.

"Boston is a nice town."

"Nice, but far away," Garren said, wiping his mouth with the back of his hand. "I'll miss him, Herbie."

"He'll miss you, too."

"Do you really think so? Even with his new job and new friends? What if he finds a new . . . new girlfriend?"

"He'll never find a new son, kid. Ever. Besides, you'll like visiting Boston. They have some great sports teams. Let's see . . ." Herbie scratched his head through his halo. "There's the Cowboys and the Bulls."

"That's the Bruins and the Celtics." Garren smiled.

"Right!" Herbie said. "All those humans in uniforms look alike to me."

"I–I don't want to see him go."

"Good-byes are never easy, kid. I ought to know." Herbie cleared his throat nervously. "Guardian angels are always moving on to other jobs."

It took Garren a minute to understand what Herbie was saying. "Don't you run out on me, too, Herbie! Don't you dare leave me all alone!"

"Hey, you're not all alone. You've got your mom and dad who love you. And friends like Elise and Ears, and Jennifer and Mosier. You've got your church, and you'll make new friends at wrestling camp and summer league. And then there's the Boss. His door is always open."

Garren gripped the handle of his book bag. "I need you, Herbie! Who else could need you half as much as I do?" Then, without looking back, Garren hurried into homeroom.

The postcard was in Garren's mailbox when he got home. It was a picture of Boston Commons. On the back was this message: "Dear Kermit, Warm up the record player!"

Garren sat on the steps of the porch and read the card over and over. Kermit? He remembered how he'd teased Elise, telling her his voice sounded more like Kermit the Frog than it did Clint Eastwood. And what about the record player? Slowly, it dawned on him. He looked over at Herbie, who was sitting quietly on the lid of the mailbox.

"Herbie, does this mean . . ."

Herbie nodded, his smile the brightest Garren had ever seen it. "The operation. It worked."

"Whoop-ee!" Garren leaped off the porch and over the peonies. "Elise can hear! She can really hear! Oh, Herbie! I've got to take her to the lake. And music. We'll fill our pockets with change and play every new song on the pizza parlor juke box. Oh my gosh, Herbie! She won't have to go to the school for the hearing impaired anymore. And my baseball games. She can come watch me play this summer. She'll love Ears's sense of humor!" Garren was still laughing as he unlocked the front door and went inside.

"Herbie," Garren said, combing his wet hair. "Do you remember Robert Coy in my second grade class?"

Herbie frowned. "Chubby. Sat in the third row."

"Uh-huh. I was thinking about him when I was in the shower just now. He had this horrible habit of checking out every cool book that came into our school library. But he didn't just keep it a week. Sometimes he'd keep it all semester, telling us about the neat pictures or stories, but never giving anybody else a shot at having the book themselves."

Herbie looked closely at Garren. "So?"

"So," Garren said, tossing the comb on the dresser and turning back his bedspread, "I don't want to be like Robert Coy. Hogging the good stuff for myself, not sharing . . . you . . . with other kids." Garren stretched out on top of his covers. "So, when are you . . . you know . . . leaving?"

"Soon. But I hate long good-byes. I'd rather just flutter away."

"How will I know when you're gone?"

Herbie shrugged. "You'll know, kid. But don't worry about that yet. I'll be around for as long as you need—really need—me."

Garren lay in the darkness, wondering how long that would be.

Chapter

31

The *ping* of the gas pump sounded outside Dad's open window. "That'll be twenty dollars even," the attendant said. Dad handed him the bill and pulled back into traffic.

"It's a long drive to Boston, isn't it?" Garren asked as he and Dad headed toward home.

"Over nine hundred miles! Hope Betsy here makes it! She's got a hundred thousand miles on her now." Dad patted the dashboard of his old Chevy. "Soon as I get settled, I'm going to look at new cars. How do you think your old man would look in a Jag? Or maybe a Cadillac?"

"Good." Garren grinned. "Real good."

"And when you visit me next month, we'll cruise down the East Coast in it. What do you say to that?"

You'll probably have a business meeting, Garren thought. But aloud he said, "That'd be swell, Dad."

All too soon they turned onto Ridge Street and stopped in front of Garren's house. Dad switched off the engine and sat there, jangling the car keys and looking down at his hands.

This is hard on him too, Garren thought. He reached inside his shirt pocket and took out the Warren Dunes picture. "Here, I brought this for you. Found it when I was going through some albums. Thought you might . . . you know . . . want it."

Dad reached for the picture and looked at it for a long time. "Warren Dunes. I remember that day. As near to perfect as any day could be."

He remembered!

"Thanks, Son."

"I'll just stick it up here for you." Garren turned down the sun visor and a battered card fell into his lap. The valentine! The valentine he'd sent Dad!

Dad looked embarrassed. "I read it sometimes. When I need a boost. When the road gets lonely."

Garren placed the picture inside the card and put them back in the sun visor. So Dad did like the valentine. So much he'd kept it where he could see it often. Garren smiled and patted the visor. He felt like a little piece of him was going to Boston with Dad.

Dad looked toward the empty house. "Your mother working?" Garren nodded. "You going to be okay?"

"Sure. I'm supposed to go talk to the manager at the apartment complex about mowing for him. I can use the money for wrestling camp. And maybe a new mitt. Then Ears is coming over later, and we're going to go sign up for summer league."

"Send me a schedule so I can call you after every game."

"And I'll give you a play-by-play, just like always." Garren reached for the door handle. "Guess I'd better be go—"

But before Garren could get out of the car, Dad pulled him across the seat and hugged him. Hard. Garren could feel Dad's heart beating, his strong arms around him. He could smell the musky sweetness of his aftershave.

Remember this. Remember how this feels.

When Dad finally pulled away, there were tears in his eyes. "Better get going before the freeway traffic gets too bad," he said, reaching under his seat for the road map.

"Yeah. Sure." Carren got out and leaned down to take one more look at Dad through the open window. "Take care of yourself. Drive careful."

The tears were gone now, and Dad gave Garren one of his great grins. "Sure thing, sport. Talk to you soon!"

And with a honk and a wave, Dad was gone.

Chapter 32

The boys roamed up and down the aisles of the mall sporting goods store. "Let's go look at pads," Ears said.

"What for?" Garren slipped on a new baseball glove.

"For my elbows and knees! My pads are worn through. Every time I wipe out, I lose three layers of skin." Ears took the glove off Garren's hand and tried it on his own. "Course you wrestlers wouldn't understand the need for protection. After all, everybody knows you're 'too tough to hurt.'"

"Only on the mat," Garren said, placing the glove back on the shelf. "Only on the mat."

"I'll meet you at the front of the store in ten minutes," Ears said, heading toward a section displaying wildly painted skateboards.

Garren strolled down the aisles, looking at fishing lures and footballs, until he came to the shoe department. This was one of Dad's accounts—had been one of Dad's accounts. Garren looked at the shoes, all lined up in neat rows, their white laces gleaming like teeth in a toothpaste commercial. His own frayed lace hung against the scuffed leather of his high-top. He remembered that day, months ago, when he'd first noticed it in Mrs. Adney's office. *Why haven't I bought new laces?* And then he knew. It was because he, too, had felt battered and frayed and pulled apart.

Suddenly Garren turned and walked straight to the wall display. He chose a new pair of shoestrings—wide and white, with perfectly rolled ends. It was time.

And as he pocketed his change, Garren heard—from far, far away—the familiar sound of tinkling wind chimes.